POISON-SPICED CUPCAKES

EMILY JAMES

STRONGHOLD BOOKS

This is a work of fiction. I made it up. You are not in my book. I probably don't even know you. If you're confused about the difference between real life and fiction, you might want to call a counselor rather than a lawyer because names, characters, places, and incidents in this book are a product of my twisted imagination. Real locales and public names are sometimes used for atmospheric purposes. Any resemblance to actual people, living or dead, or to businesses, companies, events, and institutions is completely coincidental.

Editor: Christopher Saylor at www.saylorediting.wordpress.com/services/

Cover Design: Mariah Sinclair at www.mariahsinclair.com

Published April 2021 by Stronghold Books

Ebook ISBN 978-1-988480-31-2; Print Book ISBN 978-1-988480-32-9

ALSO BY EMILY JAMES

Maple Syrup Mysteries

Sapped: A Maple Syrup Mysteries Prequel

A Sticky Inheritance

Bushwhacked

Almost Sleighed

Murder on Tap

Deadly Arms

Capital Obsession

Tapped Out

Bucket List

End of the Line

Slay Bells Ringing

(also contains a Cupcake Truck Mystery novella)

Rooted in Murder

Guilty or Knot

Stumped

Cupcake Truck Mysteries

Sugar and Vice

Dead Velvet Cake

Gum Drop Dead

A Sampling of Murder

Poison-Spiced Cupcakes

Cat and Mouse WhoDunIt

Coming Late 2021!

FREE TIPS FOR AMAZING CUPCAKES

Each book in the Cupcake Truck Mysteries includes a cupcake recipe, but even when you have a great recipe, baking the perfect cupcake can sometimes be hard.

To receive the top 10 tips for amazing cupcakes (inspired by the Cupcake Truck Mysteries sleuth, Isabel), sign up for my newsletter at www.subscribepage.com/cupcakes.

(If you're already a member of my newsletter, and you can't find the link, send me an email!)

1

Scott burst back into the bakery kitchen. The door banged against the wall and bounced back.

My arm reacted before I could stop myself. I flung the zester.

Scott sidestepped it with ease, and the door swished shut. He held his hands up. "It's just me."

Heat blazed up the back of my neck and into my cheeks. Normal people didn't throw things at their landlord-employees, no matter how surprised they were.

But Scott would probably be the last person to blame me. After what had happened here only a few months ago with the death of his father and the attack on both of us, he was jumpier than usual, too. My business partner Claire had dropped a metal bowl earlier this week, and Scott had hit the ground as if someone had shot at him.

"Next time," Scott moved out of the doorway, "at least throw a knife. A zester's like giving your attacker a paper cut."

I hadn't had a knife, and it wasn't like I'd thought it through.

Scott bent down and picked up the zester. He dropped it in the sink full of dirty dishes, knowing I wouldn't use it to continue zesting my lemons for my lemon curd without washing it first.

I moved to the sink. "I thought you'd left for the night."

I probably should have asked him to stay instead of telling him to go. Dan hated the idea of me being alone anywhere right now. Not only was I supposed to testify at the Glover murder trial in two weeks, but the date had been set for my divorce hearing. By Christmas, I'd either be divorced or dead.

But we'd closed a half hour ago, and I had prep work to do for the murder mystery weekend we were catering in a few days. Scott hadn't learned how to make curds yet, so he couldn't even help. Asking him to stay had felt like admitting I needed a babysitter. Besides, if Jarrod came for me, he wouldn't hesitate to kill Scott too. I wouldn't take that risk. Scott was already in therapy because of what we'd gone through a few months ago.

Scott hadn't replied to my comment. I pulled my hands out of the soapy water and looked at him.

His face was the pale color of unbaked cookie dough. "There's a man hanging around outside the store."

My heart felt like it did a double beat in my chest. I wouldn't jump to conclusions. "Did you tell him we're closed?"

"Not exactly." Scott rubbed a hand underneath the edge of his sweater collar. "I asked him what he was doing. I know that could turn away a customer, but I didn't want to take chances."

If I'd been anyone else, I probably would have hugged him or known what to do to console him. But I wasn't a hugger. And I was the last person you'd want giving you a pep talk.

"What did he say?" At least my voice sounded calmer than I felt. It almost sounded like I was saying something as simple as *beat the eggs.*

Scott's leg jittered. "That he was waiting for his wife to come out because he needed to talk to her."

The zester slipped from my fingers and hit the floor again with a clatter-splat.

Would Jarrod be that bold? To walk right up to my store and demand to speak with me. He might, if it served his plan more than subterfuge would.

No jumping to conclusions, remember? the logical side of my brain reminded me.

The guy out front might simply have the wrong shop. He might legitimately think his wife worked here, and he was picking her up after her shift. That was possible too.

I scooped up the zester again. "What did he look like?" The casual tone I'd been going for fell flat. My voice shook instead.

Scott's foot stopped bobbing momentarily, then started up again. "Dark hair, silver at the temples." He put his hands up to the sides of his head, miming what he'd said. "A little taller than you. He looked like he'd been in a tanning bed in the last few days. No white guy in Michigan in December is that golden."

I had to think this through. Dark hair could be Jarrod, but the last time I'd seen him, he hadn't had any gray in his hair. Still, a lot could change in a person in a couple of years.

No one in Michigan was that tanned, Scott had said. The Florida sun ensured Jarrod was always tanned.

The height was wrong, though. Jarrod was tall. Much taller than me.

I needed to see the man to be sure.

I tiptoed to the kitchen door. Which was silly. It wasn't like he could hear me. Scott would have locked the door after himself, so it wasn't like the man had gotten inside.

I eased the door open. The man outside had his face pressed almost to the glass of the window, as if he were peering in, trying to catch a glimpse of whoever he'd come to see.

I jerked back instinctively.

"Do you know him?" Scott asked.

I gave my mind a minute for the adrenaline to clear. My panic sensors weren't flaring, so my body must know, even from that flash of sight, that it wasn't Jarrod.

I cracked the door again. The man had moved back from the window slightly now. He looked familiar. I'd definitely seen him before. Was he a customer?

That didn't feel right. I motioned for Scott to follow me and walked out into the front of the shop.

The man straightened completely and waved at me.

Mike. He was Claire's ex-husband Mike. I'd only seen him a couple of times, but there was no mistaking the too-smooth smile on his face.

He shouldn't be here anymore than Jarrod should, though his presence was less dangerous.

He'd probably come to tell Claire he'd be late with her alimony again. She'd finally gotten her divorce, but Mike was known for finding creative ways to continue torturing her. His latest was to withhold her alimony payments until she had to threaten to take him to court. Then he'd pay, but in a way that created a hassle for her.

One time, he'd brought her a payment in loose change. Not rolled change. He'd actually brought a bucket of coins. And Claire couldn't do anything about it because he'd paid.

"Do you know him?" Scott whispered, more insistently this time.

I sighed. "Yes, but he's not dangerous." I glanced back over my shoulder. Claire and Scott didn't have the same friendship that Scott and I had. She probably wouldn't want him knowing all her personal business. "I'll get rid of him. Do you mind washing that zester up for me?"

"Are you sure?" Scott's feet pointed back toward the kitchen while his torso stayed angled toward the front door, as if he wanted to obey my request but wasn't convinced the man outside was safe yet. "If you're not..."

I easily finished his sentence in my mind. If I wasn't sure, we could call the police. Or we could call Dan.

Mike wasn't a threat to me, though. "I'm sure."

Scott disappeared into the kitchen. I unlocked the front door.

Mike pushed his way in before I could step out. "Is Claire in the kitchen?"

He'd gotten too close for my comfort when he stepped inside. My heart beat so fast it was almost painful in my chest. He might be Claire's ex-husband, but he was still a man. He was still bigger and stronger than me.

I took a step back, putting space between us and blocking his path to the kitchen at the same time. "She's not here, and you shouldn't be either."

He tilted his head to one side. "Are you her girlfriend?" He held his hands up as if I'd accused him of something. "No judgment. I just heard you two were living together, and she's turned down all my attempts to set her up with some great guys, so I figured..."

He shrugged like it was the most natural conclusion in the world.

My tongue felt like it'd been paralyzed by shock. Of all the things I'd expected Mike to say, accusing Claire and I of being a couple hadn't even been on the list.

What must it have been like for Claire to be married to this man for so many years?

She'd still be married to him now if he hadn't cheated on her.

He'd never done anything that could technically be called abuse, and so Claire had stayed. She believed the only grounds for divorce were abuse, adultery, and abandonment. She called them *the three A's.*

I sucked in a slow breath through my nose. I would be the bigger person here. I'd be polite to this man if it took every patient bone in my body. "Claire and I are friends and business partners, but we're not dating."

"You sure?" He moved as if he wanted to nudge me in the ribs with his elbow and then thought better of it. He tucked his elbow back into his side. "Same-sex marriage is legal in Michigan, you know."

"I'm sure. I have a husband." One I was trying to get rid of, but Mike didn't have the right to know that.

He shrugged his shoulders again. "So did Claire. That doesn't mean anything." He leaned to the side. "You're sure she's not here?"

As if I was so stupid I'd forget if Claire was back in the kitchen? If it hadn't been for the fact that I'd also been deceived and married a man who'd turned out to be the opposite of a good guy, I'd have wondered what Claire could have seen in him.

"I'm sure she's not here."

Mike moved over to one of the tables and pulled out a chair. He didn't sit. Was he expecting me to sit?

He nodded at the chair. I stayed put.

He pushed it back in. "Look, I wanted to talk to Claire about a man who started working with me. He's a widower, and he loves to garden, just like Claire. I think they'd have a lot in common."

Mike adjusted the zipper on his jacket as if he found it too warm in the shop. "She's not taking my calls anymore, and I thought this was too important to leave a message."

Good for Claire. When Mike had first abandoned her to move in with his girlfriend, he'd left boxes of his belongings in the house. He'd come back periodically to get one. Claire hadn't been brave enough to stop him until Dan took a cousin's prerogative and stepped in to do it for her. Facing Mike was the only area where Claire wasn't forceful.

Hearing she'd taken another step in protecting herself from his poor treatment made me smile inside. Both of us were finally doing what we needed to in order to be free of men who misused us.

The rest of what Mike had said sunk in. "Suggesting she accept a blind date was important enough for you to stalk her?"

The words were out of my mouth before I realized how confrontational they sounded. Maybe I'd come a long way too. I would never have had the courage to stand up to a man this way when I first came to Lakeshore. Dan would be proud of me when I told him.

Scott stuck his head out of the kitchen. "Everything okay out here?"

I must have raised my voice more than I realized. I gave him a thumb's up and turned back to Mike. He still owed me an answer.

He looked away. "That's not the only reason I wanted to talk to her. I also wanted to tell her in person that I'm getting remarried." His voice picked up speed and excitement. "But now that I think about it, it'd be much better coming from you. You could encourage Claire to agree to a date when my friend calls."

He stepped toward me, his hands moving as he talked.

I might have come a long way, but I still didn't allow most men within my personal space bubble. I stepped back and held up a hand in a *stop* gesture.

Mike stopped, but he kept looking at me like he expected me to be onboard with his idea merely because he'd suggested it. As if it should be enough that he said it.

I'd been the type of woman once who would go along with what a man said without questioning it, but only because Jarrod had controlled every aspect of my life.

I planted my hands on my hips in what I hoped was a passable impression of Claire. "I don't think she's going to go on a date just to please you."

"You wound me." He pressed a hand over his heart. "All I want is for Claire to be happy again, the way I am. That makes me a good guy. Not a bad one."

I highly doubted his motives were that pure. If he wanted Claire to be happy, he wouldn't have done all the things he'd done to her, including refusing to divorce her simply to avoid paying alimony. He'd fought the divorce even though he'd already left Claire for the woman he was now engaged to.

Claire's happiness didn't seem to rank high on his list.

Mike zipped his jacket up to the top and backed toward the door. "So I'll leave those bits of news up to you then. Thanks so much, Iris."

He was gone before I could even correct him about my name.

2

"Your apron is crooked." Claire ran her gaze over my maid's costume. "But otherwise you look like you stepped right out of the 1920s."

I adjusted the ties on my apron. Claire's matching outfit looked like she donned one every day. Her apron was so perfectly smooth that I suspected she'd stayed up last night to iron it.

I hadn't starched and ironed my costume, but I was presentable enough considering Claire and I didn't have speaking parts in the murder mystery weekend we were catering for the police department. The officers in charge of organizing this year's gathering had decided they should do something other than the traditional holiday party and Secret Santa exchange. They'd wanted to do a fun event for everyone's families.

We'd already been hired on to cater before the idea morphed

into a murder mystery weekend. Changing the event meant changing our menu. We'd come up with classic flavors that were popular during the early decades of the 1900s. Cupcakes that imitated pineapple upside down cake with pineapple compote in the center and brown butter cherry buttercream on the top. Neapolitan cupcakes where I put a brownie base under a strawberry jam-filled cupcake and topped it with vanilla Swiss meringue. I'd even invented a tomato soup and spice cupcake that replaced the dairy with canned tomato soup as a nod to a cake that was popular during the Great Depression.

All of us—Dan, Janie, Claire, and I—had been looking forward to this weekend for months. The only way it could have been better was if it'd come after Ms. Glover's trial and my divorce hearing so that I didn't have either of those casting dark shadows on the day.

Claire hurried out of the ladies' room before I could say anything else. I still hadn't told her that Mike showed up at our bakery, let alone what he said. We'd been so busy preparing for this weekend that every time I asked her if we could talk, she'd brushed me off with a *later*.

Knowing what I knew added another weight to my shoulders. Mike shouldn't have put this on me. It wasn't like we were friends or ever would be friends. I barely knew him, and I intended to keep it that way.

I trailed after Claire. The ballroom where the department

had set up the event now looked like it'd been pulled straight out of a history book.

Detective Austen, who'd been a thorn in my foot during the last murder case I'd found myself in the middle of, stood in the center of the ballroom giving last minute instructions, her sequined flapper dress catching the light. Dan's best friend Zee, dressed in a striped zoot suit that made him look like a member of Al Capone's gang, grabbed her from behind, spun her around, and kissed her. Instead of slapping him, she laughed as if it were completely normal.

I barely swallowed down an *oohhh*. That explained why Detective Austen had been willing to overlook my fake name during the last investigation. She hadn't only done it as a favor to Dan. She'd done it because Dan was her boyfriend's best friend. No wonder she'd resented me when she'd been interviewing me about the murder. She'd felt like she'd been placed in a bad position because of a relationship she had. Her reaction had still been over the top, but it made more sense now.

I was apparently going to learn a lot about Dan's colleagues this weekend by watching them interact with their families and with each other outside of a work environment.

More people streamed into the ballroom. I hurried to catch up with Claire. It was show time.

I WEAVED THROUGH THE CROWD, OFFERING MY APPETIZERS TO the guests. Claire had done the same with the savory elements as I had with the sweet ones, seeking out recipes from the beginning of the century. My current tray held cucumber canapes, salmon mousse cups, and miniature derby hot browns, an open-faced sandwich on pumpernickel bread with turkey, bacon, and tomato topped in a cheese sauce.

The members of the police department stood out, even though everyone was in some level of costume. Not only were their costumes better, but seeing them stand among people who hadn't trained at a police academy, the difference was obvious. They held their bodies wider, their arms further away from their torsos, as if trying to take up more space. Maybe they were. Maybe it was part of what had always made me nervous around them. Jarrod had stood the same way, demanded the same space.

I glanced at Dan. In comparison, he held his body like all the civilians. Which made sense. Before his brother and sister-in-law died and left him Janie, he'd worked undercover. He would have needed to retrain himself. He couldn't have the way he stood scream *cop*. Perhaps, even now, it contributed to why I'd been able to let my guard down around him.

He caught my gaze and touched two fingers to the rims of his fake spectacles in a salute. He'd landed the role of doctor.

A woman to my left gasped. I froze and spun. My tray tilted in my grip, and I righted it a second before the angle would have become steep enough to dump everything on the ground.

A man who looked to be in his late twenties sank to his knees. The crowd seemed to flow back from him. He dropped his cup, and the red liquid spilled across the floor.

My fingers clenched around my tray, and I drew in a few deep breathes, letting them out equally slowly. It was an act. It was all part of the weekend.

My brain knew it, but my instincts kept wanting to kick in.

The man made a gurgling noise and sank the rest of the way to the floor.

"He needs help!" a woman's voice shrieked. "Is there a doctor in the house?"

My pulse dropped, and a giggle tried to bubble up. Had they each written their own lines? *Is there a doctor in the house?* really did feel like it should have been pulled from an old black-and-white movie.

The crowd parted for Dan. He dropped to his knees and pressed his fingers into the man's neck.

"He's dead."

The words were so solemn that a shiver zipped up my body.

The woman who'd called for a doctor wailed.

"Everyone needs to stay put until the police arrive," Dan said.

A tiny girl—Janie's age but more fragile looking—squeezed her way between the adults legs. Janie followed behind her.

Dan was still giving his speech, his words spoken loudly enough that even the people at the back of the crowd could hear.

The little girl dropped to all fours and crawled the last few feet. She stuck her head down at the same level as the dead man. He opened one eye and winked at her. She giggled and scrambled back to Janie.

"Yup," her tiny voice carried farther than it should have for her size. "He's dead."

The real fun of the weekend had now begun.

DAN CAME INTO THE KITCHEN A FEW HOURS LATER CARRYING two chairs. "I thought you might need to rest your feet."

It would have been out of character for me to rest in the ballroom where the murder mystery weekend was taking place, but there weren't any places in sit down in the kitchen area.

I dropped into a curtsy. "Thank you, Doctor, sir." I'd tried all day for a British accent like in *Downton Abbey*, but I only ended up sounding like I'd just had dental work done.

I abandoned the accent. "It's probably a good thing I don't have a speaking role."

Dan flashed me one of his full grins, the one that sent laugh lines out from his eyes and warmth spiraling through my belly. "We aren't all meant for the stage." His smile slipped. "Have you managed to talk to Claire about the uninvited visitor the other night?"

I shook my head. "She keeps saying she's too busy, and we'll talk later. It's like she senses she won't like what I have to say."

"She might. She always senses when Janie's done something she shouldn't."

I hadn't done something I shouldn't, but she certainly wasn't going to like to hear that her ex-husband showed up at our place of business, was getting remarried, and wanted to set her up on dates.

Honestly, I wasn't sure which would make her more angry.

"At this point, I think I need to wait until the weekend is over."

Dan leaned over the cupcakes waiting for me to load them onto serving platters. The hotel had provided serving staff to assist Claire and I, but they weren't supposed to load the trays themselves, only pick them up and take them out. Claire and I had been taking turns as the person who stayed behind in the kitchen to reload. My shift in the back had just begun.

"Wait for sure," he said. "She's been talking about nothing but this weekend for a long time. Telling her about Mike now would spoil it for her."

Withholding the information on purpose felt dishonest somehow. Claire might or might not thank me for it when she found out. But it was the right call. She couldn't change what Mike was doing by knowing now or knowing two days from now.

Hopefully, Mike didn't send his "great match" friend off to find Claire and ambush her before I was able to warn her. We should be relatively safe here. Scott was manning the shop along with the new high school girl we'd hired, and Scott would make sure Abby didn't tell any visitors where we were either.

"What varieties are these again?" Dan asked.

I gave him my prepared speech. He grabbed one and came over to the stool beside me.

Dan said something, but I missed it. He'd picked a Neapolitan cupcake, but it smelled wrong. It should have smelled like chocolate, strawberry, and vanilla. Instead, it smelled like bitter almonds.

One of Jarrod's stories about a case he'd worked flashed through my mind. I couldn't remember the details anymore. I did remember one thing.

There was a poison that smelled like bitter almonds.

Dan lifted the cupcake toward his mouth. I slapped it out of his hand without stopping to think.

The cupcake spiraled through the air and landed upside down on the floor. The icing splatted out, looking like a child's dropped ice cream cone.

Some of the icing covered my fingers. I frantically wiped it on my apron. Jarrod hadn't said if this poison could be absorbed through the skin or had to be eaten. Or maybe he had. After a while, all his stories had sounded the same, with him as the hero, and I'd only paid enough attention to make the appropriate impressed noises. Why hadn't I paid more attention?

Dan's hand was still slightly raised as if we'd been playing a game of freeze tag. "Care to explain?"

I lunged toward him. "Do you have any icing on you?"

Dan shook his head. I grabbed his hand and wiped it on a clean portion of my apron anyway.

He stood and took hold of my upper arms. His touch was gentle enough that my brain didn't panic, but firm enough that I couldn't keep moving.

"What's going on?"

"The cupcake smelled wrong."

Dan's eyebrows rose. "So you had to whack it out of my grip to protect me from a bad flavor combination?"

"It smelled like bitter almonds. Isn't there a poison that smells like bitter almonds?"

Dan stilled. His gaze slid to the cupcake tray. "Cyanide."

That's what it was. Jarrod had said that not everyone could smell it.

"But is it possible you used almond extract by accident?" Dan asked.

Grabbing a wrong ingredient was always possible. So was forgetting an ingredient. But with extracts, you could smell the difference as soon as you uncapped the bottle. You'd have to be in a fugue state to accidentally substitute almond extract for vanilla extract.

"No." The word felt like it was stuck in my throat. "No."

Dan sprinted for the door. "Call 9-1-1."

He didn't have to tell me why. Some of the cupcakes from this batch had already gone out into the crowd.

I chased after him, dialing as I went.

A scream echoed through the main room. I dashed through the door.

The crowd was acting the same way they had for the first "murder" of the day.

"Let the Doc through," a man's voice said. His words ended on a chuckle.

The distinction between the officers and the civilians became about more than body language. While the civilians drew back slightly to give the actors room, the members of the police department were moving in the same direction as Dan—toward the sound. Toward the body already convulsing on the floor. Toward a person whose collapse wasn't part of the script for the weekend.

The next murder wasn't scheduled to take place until later in the afternoon. This one was real.

Claire grabbed my arm. "What's happening?"

The 9-1-1 operator came on, asking what my emergency was. Even though the room was packed with police officers, I was the only person other than Dan who knew what was happening. Dan needed to help the person who'd collapsed. I needed to make sure no one else did.

I shoved the phone at Claire. "Tell them we need ambulances. Cyanide poisoning."

Claire barely caught my phone as I released it. I couldn't slow down. So many people had cupcakes in their hands. Who knew how many of those contained poison?

I clambered up onto a table. "Don't eat anything," I yelled.

The mood in the room had shifted, as if people had suddenly started to realize this wasn't part of the program. Many of them were talking. Others had pulled out their cell phones, probably to call 9-1-1 as well. Half the people didn't seem to hear me.

Detective Labreck, the man who'd investigated the death of Dan and Claire's grandfather, appeared beside the table. For a second, I thought he was going to haul me down as if I were a crazy woman.

"Did the food cause this?" he asked.

I nodded.

"I need everyone to set down what they're eating." Labreck's voice boomed out, carrying over all the other noise. The room hushed except for the people still talking into their phones to 9-1-1. "And proceed in an orderly fashion to the restrooms to wash your hands."

A few of the other officers moved into motion, directing the family members as if they were simply working crowd control at an event.

I moved against the tide, forcing my mind to focus on getting to Dan rather than on the crush of people, the crush of men so close around me. Detective Labreck somehow managed to get in front of me. He parted the crowds, and we passed through. For whatever reason he'd decided to help me, I was grateful.

Dan knelt on the floor next to a large body in a striped suit, holding the person on their side. Detective Austen held the man's head in her lap, preventing it from banging against the floor as he seized.

I would have recognized the man anywhere. It was Zee.

3

*C*laire and I sat side by side in the nearly empty ballroom. Or, at least, nearly empty compared to how it'd been less than an hour ago. Crime scene techs had taped off the kitchen, and boxes of what remained of our food trundled past as they carried it out.

Two of the officers who'd had to stay on duty rather than attending the murder mystery weekend had arrived shortly after the ambulance. They were taking statements from the people who'd witnessed Zee's collapse. Claire and I were waiting for our turn. Based on the smell of bitter almond from the cupcake I'd stopped Dan from eating, we knew how Zee ingested the poison.

Whoever ended up investigating this case would want our statements. Likely we'd be brought back in for more interviews later as well.

My mind kept seeing Zee on the floor and superimposing

Dan's face over his. Had I not been there, had I not been able to smell the bitter almond scent, had I acted a second later, Dan could have been the one to die.

I couldn't even make that feel real.

Dan had almost died from a cupcake I baked.

Claire stared off at the wall, as if she didn't see anything happening around us, and her legs bounced under the table. The table shuddered with the force of it.

She clamped my hand in hers. My bones moved painfully, but I didn't pull away. The human touch felt grounding somehow. As if, without it, my mind might float away and not come back.

"I made that batch." Claire's voice had the same shake to it as her body. "I made it and iced those cupcakes this morning because you were running behind."

Poor Claire. She'd been through a lot lately. Her husband leaving her. Her grandfather dying and her little cousin almost being murdered. Opening her home to me, with all the danger that brought. Witnessing a murder, and then having our landlord turn up dead in our bakery right before we were supposed to open.

She'd once asked how Dan managed to do his job. He saw so much evil, but he kept fighting against it every day instead of giving up. Most people couldn't experience that much tragedy without it breaking something inside them. It was why police officers had such a high incidence of alcoholism and suicide.

Dan and I were very much alike.

Dan kept going because he believed that God could bring good out of any situation. I kept going because it was my way of standing up for people who couldn't stand up for themselves. I'd once been the one who couldn't stand up for herself and who had no one to stand up for her.

If Claire continued to experience tragedy, she'd find her own way through it as well. In the meantime, I'd help her however I could.

I squeezed Claire's hand in return. "This wasn't your fault. You didn't put cyanide in the food."

Claire made a huffing noise. "Of course not. Not intentionally anyway." She lifted her gaze to meet mine. Her eyes were wide, as if she were still expecting something else bad to happen. "I'm so grateful I made that icing. You always lick the bowl to test the quality of each batch. I never lick the bowl. Too many calories adding up. If you'd made it..." Her voice broke.

My heart felt like it was beating so hard it was rattling my bones. She was right. I would have tasted it. I especially would have tasted it if it didn't smell right because I'd think I'd accidentally grabbed a bottle of almond extract that had something wrong with it rather than the vanilla that belonged in the recipe.

I'd be dead. "We don't know the poison was in the icing rather than in the batter."

Claire's skin paled to a shade that belonged only on corpses. "We do. We had Janie when you were baking that batch. I remember because I gave her a lecture about eating raw batter after she ran a finger around the inside of the bowl once you'd scooped the batter out into the baking tins."

My throat burned and my head felt even more disconnected from my body than it had a moment before. Janie had sneaked a taste of that batter. I'd promised her she could try a baked one instead, and it would taste so good she'd never want to eat the batter raw again. She'd eaten an entire cupcake from this batch. If the cyanide were in the cupcake rather than in the icing, Janie would already be dead.

Blackness fuzzed at the edges of my vision. Had one small thing gone differently, I could have lost any of the people who meant the most to me. I lowered my forehead to the table.

Claire rested her free hand on the top of my head. It felt like what a mother or big sister would have done at a time like this. Claire had become the closest I'd ever had to either.

"Maybe it's good the bakery is shut down for a few days," Claire said.

Despite what had happened to one of their own—or maybe because of it—the officers had mobilized rapidly. Our bakery and house were off limits as they searched for the cyanide. All the products in our store would need to be tested or disposed of.

For all we knew at this point, it was another Tylenol murderer case where the culprit had laced Tylenol with cyanide and then let people buy it off the store shelves. We might have bought supplies laced with cyanide. The police would know once they tested the rest of our materials. If that were the case, it'd cause mass panic when the police had to recall all the powdered sugar or unsalted butter.

"How can we know that this won't happen again?" Claire's voice had taken on a wobbly tone. "How can I ever feel safe baking again?"

Those were valid questions to add to the growing list. Unfortunately, I didn't have the answer to those either.

4

_D_etective Labreck stood in the doorway of the room they were using for interviews until I picked a seat at the table. The table was round, so I didn't see that it made much of a difference where I sat.

He closed the door and selected a seat that wasn't directly across from me, which could have felt adversarial, but wasn't so close that we'd feel like friends having a chat.

His movements looked like a sigh sounded, slow and resigned.

I'd managed to avoid him for most of the case where I'd been a suspect in the death of Dan and Claire's grandfather. I'd only added a face to the name later.

He set down a pad of paper with the hotel's logo at the top. "Your name is Isabel Addington, correct?"

Nothing like opening with a hard one. Dan wasn't here to

smooth things over or ask for favors. This time I'd have to handle it myself.

I met Detective Labreck's gaze, even though it made my body shiver with the need to run. He'd worked the Glover case. He knew my real name. But perhaps Dan hadn't revealed to anyone other than the district attorney trying the case that Isabel Addington and Amy Miller were the same person. After all, Dan had only been brought into the case at all after it closed because "Amy" refused to deal with anyone else.

Or perhaps Detective Labreck was testing me to see if I'd lie to him. With the Glover trial coming up next week and my divorce hearing the week after that, lying about my name now seemed like an unnecessary gamble.

"I work under the name Isabel Addington, but my real name is Amy Miller."

He didn't write it down. So he had known.

The fact that he didn't write it down made me respect him more. His notes would be seen by multiple people before this case was closed, and many of those people would know there wasn't any Amy Miller invited to the party.

"Alright, Ms. Addington, start at the beginning for me and tell me what happened."

The beginning felt nebulous. I didn't know when the poison got into our food. The start for me was when I smelled bitter almond in the cupcake Dan was about to eat. I began there and went until the paramedics loaded Zee into the ambulance and Dan and Detective Austen ran off to follow in a car.

Detective Labreck jotted things down as I spoke. His letters ran together. Either he had very poor handwriting or he wrote in his own form of shorthand.

"And how long have you known Detective Garcia?"

Had someone else died? I'd heard one other person complaining of symptoms, but I thought we stopped everyone before anyone else could eat the bad batch. Only one tray had gone out. "I don't think I know Detective Garcia."

"Zee Garcia."

There was almost a sad smile in Detective Labreck's voice. I'd never met anyone before whose actions and words added so many extra messages. He was a detective, so he had to be aware of it. He probably used it to his advantage to unbalance suspects.

His style of interviewing was very different from Dan's, Detective Austen's, and the few other detectives I'd interacted with.

I probably should have known Zee's last name, but he'd always been Zee when Dan talked about him. I couldn't help feeling I'd given something away that could reflect negatively on me. I just didn't know what it might be.

"I only met him a couple of times. He runs a women's self-defense course, and Dan and I train privately in one of the other rooms of the gym at the same time. I know he's one of Dan's best friends."

What Detective Labreck wrote down this time definitely wasn't any version of English I'd ever seen. That confirmed my suspicion that he wrote in shorthand. He'd have to type all his notes up anyway for the official file, but this allowed him to write whatever he wanted without a person of interest getting an unintended look.

"And how is your relationship with Dan?" He put the tiniest emphasis on *Dan* as if to make sure that I knew he hadn't called him Detective Holmes on purpose. "Have you two been arguing or has there been any strain on the relationship lately?"

The way he said it reminded me of how spouses or significant others were questioned after their loved one was murdered. Did everyone at the department think Dan and I were a couple? We weren't. Not in the way they'd expect at least. Not yet anyway.

Heat crept up my neck and into my cheeks, and there wasn't anything I could do to stop it. Blushing about what might or might not be between Dan and I felt like something a high school girl with a crush would do, but bodies sometimes acted on their own.

Either way, Dan hadn't been the one who ate the poisoned cupcake. I could have let him eat the one in his hand had anything been wrong between us. The question felt like Labreck was abusing the situation to nurse his own curiosity. I wouldn't have expected something so unprofessional from him.

"I'm not sure how my relationship, platonic or otherwise, with Dan has any bearing on this case."

Detective Labreck laid a hand over his note pad, as if it were a microphone he wanted to block instead of paper that had to be written on. "I know you might not think so, but I'm trying to help you right now. For Dan's sake. I've known him since he came back here on the heels of losing his brother and had to adapt to a new department, a new role in his career, and single parenthood all at once. I know you mean something to him, so I'm asking all the questions someone else is going to ask when this investigation is taken out of our hands. Because it will be. This is your chance to clear things up when you have a sympathetic ear."

Oh. Overreact much, Isabel. After this was all over, Detective Labreck was getting a dozen cupcakes of his favorite flavor. "I'm just not sure how my relationship with Dan could matter to this case." I made sure to keep my tone conciliatory so Detective Labreck would know I wasn't trying to continue to argue.

"Dan and Zee have a longstanding friendship. If I were to spin that to look for a motive for you, I could say you were jealous of that relationship. I could say you and Dan had a fight, and you wanted to hurt him. I could say you and Dan were having problems and you made an error in judgment and slept with Zee, who then wanted to tell Dan."

A snort slipped out before I could stop in. I wasn't prone to snorting for any reason, but if Detective Labreck knew my history at all, he'd have known how ludicrous that last suggestion was. Setting aside that I was trying to live my Christian faith, which meant not sleeping with a man I wasn't married to, *and* setting aside that I was still married and shouldn't be sleeping with anyone who wasn't my husband, the only man who I felt comfortable being close to was Dan. Even that closeness had been hard fought. Each new step we took in the future would probably be one that we had to approach slowly and with patience on his part.

The idea that I could so easily fall into bed with a man I barely knew...

But for all that, Labreck hadn't spoken harshly or as if he were trying to push me so I'd admit something. His consideration could be an act. Still, there was a softness to his expression that made me think he wasn't acting.

"Dan and I have a complicated relationship right now." That sounded bad. Unless I wanted to lose Labreck as a potential ally, I'd have to be more forthcoming. "I'm currently trying to get out of an abusive marriage. So Dan and I don't have the relationship that we might..." My face felt like it was on fire. And there was nowhere to hide. "Complicated but good."

A smile flittered across Detective Labreck's face so fast that I almost missed it. "Alright. I have one more thing to ask you about, and then you'll be free to go."

"Ask as many as you need. You're right that I'd rather sort this out with you than with a stranger."

A stranger who might be a man who'd try to intimidate me. A stranger who might look at my past and hold it against me. The things I'd done hadn't always been legal.

"You and Detective Austen butted heads during the investigation of your landlord's death. Do you hold any animosity toward her?"

Detective Austen had seemed to dislike me from the start simply because Dan had asked her not to ask my name. She hadn't even had to bend the rules for that, let alone break them, but she'd seemed to take it as a personal insult that I'd want her to even move in the direction of the unusual.

She'd also been less than helpful when we'd thought the vandalism that happened to the store might have been connected to our landlord's death.

All that said, though, nothing she'd done was reason enough to kill her, let alone someone else.

"I didn't even know she and Zee were dating until today if that's the angle you're going for."

Another expression flashed over his face too quickly for me to interpret. For a second, I saw myself through his eyes. I was a horrible interview subject. The way I phrased things was awkward enough to make me sound guilty even when I was innocent. I hedged things to protect myself.

He was right. If this case got handed over to an outside department to investigate, they'd look closely at me, and I'd probably come out of it with a target on my back.

I had this moment to clarify. "Detective Austen was doing her job, and she was trying not to step over any lines while doing it. I respect that."

Labreck flipped his pad of paper over and stood. He swept an arm toward the door. "You're free to go. But Ms. Addington?"

I collected my purse and got to my feet as well. "Yes?"

"Think about the questions I asked and get more comfortable with your answers. I doubt this will be the last time someone asks them. You and Ms. Cartwright are both going to be suspects because you have connections to the department and had full access to the contaminated food."

In other words, if outsiders came in to investigate this case, I needed to watch my back. Dan wouldn't be able to protect me, and to outside eyes, I looked guilty in multiple different ways.

he sound of Dan's key turning in the deadbolt jerked me awake. I sat up on the couch and turned the lamp on.

Claire and Janie had gone to bed hours ago, but I didn't want Dan to come home to a house that felt empty even if it wasn't.

Soft noises came from the entry way. Two thumps that had to be him kicking off his shoes, followed by the rustle of fabric as he removed his coat.

The sounds were so ordinary that they felt out of place after a day like today.

He stepped into the doorway. For the first time since I'd met him, Dan looked older than his age. Shadows surrounded his eyes, and his whole face sagged like he'd never smile again.

I opened my arms, and he walked straight into them. He held my body with the same fierceness as Claire had held my hand earlier. He buried his face into the curve where my neck and shoulder met.

I felt like the stake to his wind-blown tree, the thing that would keep him from breaking during a time when his roots might otherwise be too weak. I'd never been that to anyone before. Hadn't thought I ever could be that to someone. The person leaning on you had to think you were strong enough to take the weight.

I moved a hand up to the back of Dan's neck and stroked the exposed skin. He shuddered.

I'd almost lost him today. I'd almost lost this man who made me feel strong. Who'd helped me to find my value again. Who'd seen something in me before I could see it in myself.

My best friend.

The person I loved most in the world.

The person whose side I wanted to stand by for the rest of my life.

The person who'd finally meant more to me than my fear of Jarrod finding me.

And I'd almost lost him today.

My grip on him tightened. "Did Zee make it?"

Dan shook his head against my neck. He pulled away slightly and brought his hands up to my face.

He ran his fingers over my cheekbones and across my skin, sending heat and sparks racing through my body. His eyes followed the path of his fingers,

"I could have lost you today. You and Janie and Claire."

His words echoed my thoughts so closely that it was like he'd heard them. They also copied Claire's sentiments from earlier. We probably wouldn't be the only people taking stock of our loved ones today and feeling a new gratitude.

For Dan, it was as bitter as sweet though. Zee was gone.

Dan straightened, took my hand, and brought me over to the couch. He sat close and looped an arm around my shoulders, as if, like Claire earlier with holding my hand, he needed to reassure himself that I was still real and alive. "What makes this even worse is our department isn't allowed to investigate. Detectives are being sent in from out of town because the governing powers don't think anyone at our station can be objective."

Whoever had made that decision wasn't wrong. Lakeshore PD had not only lost one of their own today. They'd also come face to face with what Dan, Claire, and I had. Any of the people they loved who were there could have been killed. Had we not discovered the poison when we did, more people might have eaten the cupcakes before we stopped them. As it was, only one other woman had shown any symptoms. She'd taken her first bite of a poisoned cupcake when Zee collapsed.

To take away the department's ability to do anything when their loved ones had been threatened seemed cruel. But with all the accusations being leveled at the police these days, it was also probably wise. While many members of the department—like

Dan—might have been able to still approach this with professionalism, others would have been on a witch hunt.

I couldn't blame anyone who wasn't able to maintain objectivity. When the people you loved were in danger, many were willing to do things they wouldn't otherwise do. Losing my unborn baby had been what finally gave me the push to try to escape Jarrod, after all.

The problem was that when it came to the police, if they didn't do things exactly as they should, the lapse in protocol could cost them a conviction.

I leaned against Dan, and his arm tightened around me, his body warm at my side.

His muscles were tense even as he held me close. He didn't have to tell me that he was struggling with letting this go for me to know.

When his grandfather was killed, he hadn't been allowed to work the case. At least not officially. Unofficially he'd continued to look into it. If he hadn't, we'd never have met. We also wouldn't have caught Ms. Glover, and Janie would be dead.

Thanks to Jarrod, I'd never been someone who was comfortable trusting the proper authorities to handle something. This time that was doubly true.

Someone had used me to harm Dan. Someone had used me to kill someone. I couldn't sit back and hope a person without any personal connection to the case would be as invested in solving it as I would be.

But, this time, I had to respect Dan's wishes, too. This was also his department who'd been attacked. His friend who'd died. He deserved a say in what—if anything—we did next.

I leaned my head against his shoulder. "Sometimes having a personal stake in how the case turns out makes the difference. Sometimes the official channels need help, like the parent who refuses to stop digging into the disappearance of their child long after the case has gone cold. You might not be able to look into this officially, but that doesn't mean we can't do anything. We don't have to go full vigilante, like those powers-that-be were worried about. We won't take punishment into our own hands. But we can help find enough evidence to make sure that whoever did this goes to prison."

Dan stayed so still and silent beside me that I wasn't sure what he was thinking. The only motion was the rise and fall of his chest and his fingers stroking my upper arm.

Sitting like this, we were probably flirting with lines we shouldn't while I was still married. Given what had happened, though, being close like this wasn't about romance. It was about leaning on each other for strength and comfort.

It was something I never thought I'd find. Something I never thought I'd be able to accept even if I found it. Jarrod—

I mentally shook myself. Jarrod didn't belong here. That's why I'd filed the divorce. Jarrod had taken up too much of my life even after I left. This time, this space, wasn't about Jarrod. I had to stop letting him in if I wanted to have that future Dan talked about. Assuming we both survived this case and my divorce hearing, of course.

Dan's arm squeezed me gently against his side. "We do make a great team."

He'd offered to be a team during that first case we'd worked together, and I'd thought I wasn't a team player.

It turned out I'd just needed to find the right team.

6

"*A*re you taking point on this op?" Dan asked.

His tone contained a hint of teasing and his breath brushed warm against the top of my head.

"I think I'll defer to your experience."

"The first thing I always want to know is motive, but we can't figure that out until we know the target."

Dan's hand went back to stroking my arm. Even through my sweater it was making it hard to concentrate now that we were moving away from feeling grief into taking action. I'd never had this easy, intimate closeness with Jarrod, even at the start. With him, it'd always been about control and manipulation.

This with Dan was so different. The tenderness of it was intoxicating.

I forced my mind back to what we needed to do. Spending too much time thinking about Dan's closeness right now wasn't wise. "What avenue are the outside detectives taking? We might as well consider something different."

My voice came out a little unsteady.

Dan must have been feeling something similar to what I was because he straightened and stood. "This seems like a conversation that needs coffee to help us focus."

We moved into the kitchen.

Dan set a pot to brew. "The detectives who've been called in are looking at this as a domestic terrorism attack on the department. That's part of why none of us are officially on the case. They've brought in a team that regularly works similar cases."

When I heard the words *domestic terrorism*, I didn't think about an attack on a local police force. I envisioned mass voter intimidation, assassinating the president, or bombing an important financial building on Wall Street. Maybe that was my naivete talking. "I thought domestic terrorism had to coerce civilians into doing something or affect government policy or the government's ability to function."

"The definition is a bit more fluid than that, but that's the gist of it."

The hearty aroma of coffee filled the air. It was like wrapping myself up in a warm blanket. "Then how does this qualify?"

Dan shook his head and shrugged. "They're assuming they'll find a motive that makes sense of it, like a takeover of the city that would have been possible if they'd incapacitated a large portion of the police department. Putting cyanide in your icing sugar had the potential to result in mass murder."

The warmth the smell of the coffee had brought on evaporated, leaving me feeling colder than I had before. "So they found cyanide in the icing?"

The coffee pot beeped, and Dan poured two cups. He added the right amount of milk and sugar for both of us and brought them to the table.

"In the icing on over three dozen cupcakes and counting. They also found traces of cyanide in the powdered sugar bag that Claire threw away in the trash at the hotel."

At least they wouldn't be looking at Claire and I as suspects anymore. If we'd intentionally added the cyanide, it would have been in the icing and in the mixing bowl, but not in the bag.

"They've recalled all the powdered sugar in the city," Dan said. "But so far, it's all negative. And they're still testing samples from everything they took from the bakery. I have a lab tech friend who's keeping me in the loop."

He said it without the guilt that I would have. Even before he was planning to continue investigating on his own, he'd clearly still wanted to know what was happening.

"If they find cyanide in more of the powdered sugar from the store, then it is a terrorist attack but not one aimed at the department."

Dan nodded. "Exactly. But if it was only in your products…"

Then the target was more specific.

Claire's earlier words about her making the icing instead of me came flooding back in a rush. I felt the truth of them in my gut, like a hot bubble building.

The words I needed to say didn't want to come out. As long as I didn't say them, then I could pretend this wasn't what it was starting to look like.

But I had to. We'd be wasting time if we didn't consider it as an option.

"If the lab only finds cyanide in my supplies, then it probably wasn't about the department or the public at all." My words came out barely audible, as if my subconscious was still fighting against facing the truth. "It was probably meant for either Claire or me. Claire pointed out that the only reason I'm not dead now too is she made that batch of icing because I was running behind, and she never tastes it. I always do. Most bakers taste as they go to make sure the balance is right. Whoever put the cyanide in the powdered sugar probably thought I'd die from it long before anyone else had a chance to eat it."

Dan's gaze rested on me. His eyes moved as if he were examining every facet of my face.

He nodded slowly, like he didn't want to admit the truth of my words but had to. "Claire doesn't have any enemies that I know of who'd want her dead. So this was more likely meant for you."

The air I tried to breath in refused to re-inflate my lungs. It was one thing to think something bad and another thing entirely to hear someone else confirm it.

Dan reached across the table and brushed my fingers with his. "If it was meant for you, my guess is it's related to the Glover case again."

A few months ago, Ms. Glover's brother had tried to intimidate me into not testifying in his sister's case. He hadn't resorted to violence, but that didn't mean someone else in their family wouldn't. After all, what kind of parents raised two children like them.

I nodded to let Dan know I'd heard him.

He shifted in his seat. "You're set to testify early next week. That means the danger will be over soon. Until then, I'll buy some fresh groceries, and we'll all take an extended weekend here. We can watch some movies and play board games. Janie will think it's the best thing ever."

His inflection changed slightly on *best thing ever*. That was Janie's newest phrase when she was excited about something.

Dan's idea seemed like the smartest thing to do. Once I testified and the danger was past, we could focus on catching whoever had done this.

7

J moved far enough away from the courtroom where the Glover trial was taking place that I wouldn't undermine my testimony if anyone spotted me. Then my legs refused to move anymore. I sank to the floor, my back to the wall, shivers wracking my body.

Dan knelt beside me. "You did a great job."

Air seemed in short supply so I nodded instead.

"You really did." DA Hall stopped at my feet and looked down at me. "Showing emotion the way you did actually works in our favor. You didn't lose your temper with the questions from the defense, and you were able to clearly answer each one. That's what matters."

I nodded, but the shaking in my body made my teeth chatter together like I was in a blender. I'd stutter if I tried to form words.

Dan and Claire and I had devoted extra time the past few days while we isolated together to practicing the list of questions DA Hall made for me. The reality had been worse. Ms. Glover's defense attorney tried to paint me as a drug addict because of my time on the streets. Why else would I live in my truck? As a liar because my husband was a respected FBI agent, and there'd never been a single report of domestic abuse.

I'd known he would try to discredit me. I had the answers ready, including people who would verify my story. DA Hall had actually gone back to the church and the pastor who'd helped me escape. She'd taken written statements from him and his wife, copies of which I'd tucked away safely for my divorce proceedings.

Finally, the judge had put a stop to the defense's attacks, saying that he couldn't continue to crucify the victim. The defense attorney tried to argue he was establishing my character, and the judge had flatly told him that my character had been established, now he was badgering.

Thankfully, the defense hadn't tried to bring in Jarrod to discredit me. Maybe he knew this particular judge wouldn't allow it. Maybe Jarrod had some shred of ethical decency left and wouldn't let a murderer walk free just to hurt me.

Either way, I'd survived it, and all it'd taken was to allow myself to be cut open and filleted in front of a room full of strangers.

DA Hall looked as if she wanted to shake my hand but

couldn't find a way while she was standing and I was on the floor. "Anyway, I wanted to say thank you. I know that couldn't have been easy, but I think it made our case. The looks on the faces of the women in the jury when he tried to discredit you and you told him about losing your baby because of your husband's abuse..." She shook her head. "Every time he tried to poke a hole in your account of what happened when Ms. Glover tried to kill Janie turned the jury against him a little more. I'll text Detective Holmes when the jury comes back, but I think we've won this case in no small part thanks to you."

Dan took my hand. "Now we need to get you safely out of here."

I imagined myself as a bag of almonds scattered across a counter and slowly put each one back into the bag. Once I was safely home, I could rest. This wasn't the time or the place to let the memories overwhelm me.

I still had to get home without Jarrod waylaying me.

DA Hall did shake my hand once I was on my feet. Then she left us. The break in the proceedings had only been for fifteen minutes.

I dusted off my pants. Claire had picked out my outfit for today, as well as handling my hair and make-up this morning.

Dan leaned closer. "I know the timing is all wrong," he whispered in my ear, "but you look beautiful."

His closeness sent a good shiver down my neck, and tears burned my eyes. Beautiful. It'd been a long time since I'd felt beautiful, and an even longer time since anyone had said I was. Jarrod—

I cut the thought off before it could form. It didn't matter what Jarrod had said or thought.

I impulsively pressed a kiss to Dan's cheek. "Thank you."

A smile rose from his mouth to his eyes. "Time to go home."

The smile I'd felt growing inside withered away. This was the scariest part. This was the part where Jarrod would know where to find me and could make a move.

If he wanted to stop me from airing everything that he'd done in the divorce proceeding, it was also one of his last chances. Jarrod was not the kind of man who brooked embarrassment or humiliation. He wouldn't want the truth coming out.

The plan was Dan and I would now drive to the police station. We'd enter through the front doors, then I'd change into a uniform and exit out the backdoor with…

Zee. I was supposed to go out the backdoor with Zee, as if we were two officers leaving on a shift. Without Zee…

Dan must have noticed my expression because he squeezed my hand. "Detective Labreck will be filling in."

Detective Labreck was a good next choice. At least I'd met him before.

Dan drove the car on a circuitous route for the first few turns and then headed for the station. He parked the car in the spot he'd had reserved out front.

I waited for him to open my door and climbed out.

Raised voices came from my left, a man and a woman's. I glanced in their direction.

Detective Austen was the woman. I recognized her even though she was in jeans and not wearing her dressy clothes.

The man was Jarrod.

My heart felt like it slammed into the front of my chest, stopped, and then started again so fast I couldn't breathe.

I couldn't breathe.

I stumbled.

Dan caught me by the elbow. "Are you alright?"

Run, Fear shrieked inside my head. *Run! Run! Run!*

But Dan had my elbow, and I couldn't breathe, and Jarrod stared straight at me. There was nowhere I could run.

He was coming toward us then.

He hadn't changed in the two years since I'd last seen him, when he tried to grab me after I'd escaped and a construction worker intervened.

If you asked someone to describe an FBI agent, Jarrod would be what they imagined. Tall. Muscular. Chiseled jaw.

He still had the small scar above his eyebrow that he'd gotten when a criminal broke a beer bottle on his face during the short time we were dating. At least, that was the story he'd told me. After everything that had happened, I didn't know what was true anymore and what had been a careful script to earn my trust.

He still had the smile that made every woman he met think

he was the man of their dreams.

He still had cold eyes, if you could tear yourself away from the dazzle of his smile long enough to look. I hadn't been able to. Not soon enough anyway. Only after we were married and after the smile was gone.

I sucked in a breath, and the world popped back into motion, as if I'd been frozen in time for a moment.

Dan's glance skipped from me to Jarrod. Whatever he saw in my face, he placed his body slightly in front of mine just before Jarrod stopped next to us.

"Amy." His voice sounded like honey, golden and warm. "I thought you had your trial today. What brings you here?"

As if we were old friends. As if I told him where I'd be. As if he hadn't come here to find me.

But he couldn't have known, could he? He wouldn't do something as obvious as hang around outside a police station in December hoping I'd have a reason to come here. Or had he thought this was the likeliest plan to keep me away from him after the trial?

My mind couldn't grasp on to one idea, one thought, long enough to work it through.

Jarrod extended his hand to Dan. "FBI Special Agent Jarrod Miller. It's a pleasure to meet you in person Detective Holmes. Thank you for taking such good care of my *wife*. I wouldn't have wanted anything to happen to her before I could get here to take care of her."

The emphasis on the word *wife* was subtle but unmissable.

Dan ignored the extended hand. "I wouldn't want anything to happen to her ever."

Jarrod shifted his hand in my direction as if he hadn't meant for Dan to shake it. He'd always meant it for me. "Time to go, Amy. We don't need to take up any more of Detective Holmes' time now that the trial is over."

Spoken as if I'd been hiding here with his agreement just until I testified.

He used the voice that had always told me I needed to obey. No one else ever seemed to hear the warning in it. Or the promise of pain if I didn't do as I was told.

Something inside me felt like it cracked. What had I been thinking? It was always going to end this way. He was always going to find me and force me to go back with him. Even if I managed to divorce him, what made me think he'd give up after the divorce. He'd never give up. And if I didn't go with him now, he'd find a way to hurt me and to hurt anyone who tried to help me.

My weight shifted as if my feet were going to obey his command.

Dan's hand reached back and warm fingers wrapped around mine. My heart rate dropped slightly, and I clutched his hand as hard as I could.

Jarrod's gaze shifted with the movement. His smile hardened on his face like a gemstone. He focused his eyes on Dan. "I see she still has a taste for men in uniform. She's good at playing the damsel in distress. What story did she give you? When I met her serving tables, it was that she'd spent all her money caring for her sick dad and had nothing left to go to school. All of it turned out to be a lie to earn my sympathy and make me want to take care of her. Turned out she never mentioned school again after we got married, and she had a lot more money hidden away in a private account than she ever told me about. But she's a very good actress, so I shouldn't be surprised."

He gave Dan a smile that anyone else might have thought was sincere.

His gaze slipped back to me. "I'll see you later, darlin'."

He must have walked away because the next thing I knew he wasn't standing in front of us anymore.

Those things he'd said. They made me sound like I was the predator. That I used men in positions of authority to get what I wanted. That I was using Dan.

Some of the things he said were even true. I had money in the bank. My dad's life insurance money that I hadn't had the heart to use so soon after his death. I later used it to buy my food truck and escape Jarrod. I had wanted to go back to school, and I never did.

But I didn't go back to school because Jarrod never let me. I hid that money because it was my dad's, and I knew he'd take it for himself.

Truth twisted to sound like lies. Lies twisted to sound like truth.

Dan could easily doubt me now.

And I couldn't find words. I couldn't make them move from my head to my lips. It was like the connection was broken. I needed to say something.

Dan was still focused on Jarrod as Jarrod climbed into a car.

I yanked my phone from my purse and opened the notes app. *Please don't let him.*

I didn't know how to finish. Please don't let him take me. Please don't let him trick you. It all sounded like a weak ploy.

Jarrod's car pulled away from the curb.

Dan turned back to me. His gaze roamed my face. "You're going to be okay."

I turned my phone toward him. Something was better than nothing.

He looked at the screen, then at me again. "Is it okay if I touch you?"

Yes. I needed to feel connected and safe. I nodded.

He gently pulled me into his arms, tucking me in tight. His heart beat in my ear, and my own heart slowed to match.

"I didn't work as long as I did undercover," he said, "without knowing a liar when I see one."

I nodded against his chest.

He pulled back slightly and kissed my temple. "Give yourself time to get your words back. It can happen when you're a trauma survivor, and you've been triggered. Meeting him here with no warning was as big a trigger as we could have found."

"Dan?" a woman's voice said from behind me.

Dan didn't make a move to let me go, as if he were willing to have a conversation with someone else while holding me in his arms if that's what I needed.

As much as I wanted to stay there, I wanted to prove to myself that Jarrod couldn't break me.

I didn't move entirely out of his arms, but I shifted so that he had one arm around me instead of both and I could see the woman who'd approached us.

Detective Austen.

Her hair was pulled back into a messy ponytail, and she didn't have any make-up on. Without it, she looked washed out, her eyes both red and surrounded by swipes of purple that said she'd been up all night crying.

"What are you doing here, Miranda?" Dan's voice sounded like it did when Claire got into one of her unreasonable moments and he was talking her out of it. "I know the chief gave you a couple weeks off with pay. You should really take that time."

"He did, but..." She pulled on her hair as if realizing I was there for the first time and wanting to fix the chaos. "No one would tell me how the case was going. I thought that if I came down in person, someone might."

She stopped without saying *might take pity on her*, but it

had to be what she meant.

Dan jerked his head toward the building. "It's all outsiders. I got cut out too and told to take a week or two off."

"I know." Her gaze wandered back to the front of the station. "I've been in already. I'm not giving up, though."

Her voice had a hint of desperation to it. She and Zee hadn't been married, so she wasn't even officially entitled to any information.

My chest felt tight again. Detective Austen and I hadn't gotten along, but seeing anyone like this was hard.

"Do you know Zee's family?" Dan asked softly.

She shook her head. "Christmas. I was supposed to meet them at Christmas."

"I'll call them. Zee's mom will tell you whatever the detectives tell her, okay?"

She nodded, but the way she looked at the station said that wasn't going to be enough. Then something in her face shifted, and she swiveled to where Jarrod's car had been a few minutes ago. "The guy who just left was claiming to be a member of the FBI. He even had a badge. He was asking me a lot of questions about you." She shook her head as if it hadn't made any sense, then nodded at me. "And her. I tried to be as vague as I could, but I couldn't refuse to answer completely. Not if he turned out to actually be law enforcement. I didn't want to look like I was impeding whatever his investigation was, and he was getting... pushy about it. I wanted you to know."

8

_W_e went through with the plan. What other choice did we have.

With one small modification. I must have been less responsive than I thought because Dan and Detective Labreck decided Dan would come with Labreck and me, and a couple other officers would bring Dan's car home later. They were talking around me, the words bouncing off me. They handed me a uniform, and a female officer showed me to a room where I could change.

I almost missed Detective Austen. I didn't like her, but at least I knew her. Even though the other female officer turned her back, she was still a stranger in the room with me while I stripped to my underwear.

Besides, Detective Austen had taken the time to warn Dan that Jarrod had been asking about him.

My heart beat hard enough in my chest that it felt like it was going to leave bruises on the inside.

Jarrod hadn't been asking about me. He'd been asking about Dan.

That knowledge swirled in my head, growing bigger and bigger, as we walked out to a cruiser with Labreck, drove around town long enough to be sure we weren't being followed, and then stopped in front of Dan's house.

"You need to clear the house," I blurted.

Labreck's hands twitched on the wheel. "Excuse me?"

Dan leaned forward even though he couldn't reach me through the grate separating the front from the back. "He couldn't have followed us."

He didn't comment on the fact that I'd gotten my voice back. I could have spoken sooner, but I wanted to work it through in my own mind and make sure I wasn't being overly panicked. Now that the shock of seeing Jarrod had passed, my brain had switched from flight to bracing for what was to come. I'd always experienced an unnatural calm when I needed to take steps to protect myself from Jarrod, whether it was coming up with the right things to say or protecting my vital organs.

I swiveled in my seat, so I could see both Dan and Detective Labreck. "He wouldn't need to have followed us anymore. He asked Detective Austen questions about you. One of the first things he probably wanted was your home address. And she said she'd had to tell him what he asked because he's an FBI agent."

Dan cursed softly, something I'd only ever heard him do a handful of times. "Lock the doors as soon as we get out."

For whatever good that would do me. The glass on police cruisers wasn't bullet proof. It should have been, but it wasn't.

Dan and Detective Labreck got out. They both drew their service weapons and disappeared into the house. My muscles clenched, and my whole body ached.

This was what I'd been afraid of. This was why I hadn't wanted to get close to anyone. I'd known this would happen. My presence would put them in danger. How could I go back to Claire's house now? Claire wouldn't be up alone at night vacuuming out her stress if that happened. I'd be with her.

Dan had said he was willing to take the risk if I was. Maybe he'd thought it would be like being undercover. He'd have always been in danger on those assignments. The difference was he'd have known he could eventually come out and be back in his safe life. Now the danger was here, and nowhere was safe.

Dan and Labreck came out of the house.

Dan motioned for me to leave the car. I climbed out.

"Empty." He shook hands with Detective Labreck. "Thanks, Tom."

Detective Labreck nodded. "You two be careful until this all settles down. You have a couple weeks off just like Miranda. Make use of them." He nodded toward the house. "I'll wait here until you get inside."

Dan had me walk in front of him up the steps and into the house, as if he didn't want to let me out of his sight.

We turned the deadbolt on the door. The snap wasn't as reassuring as it should have been. Jarrod knew how to pick locks.

The collar of the police uniform I'd borrowed suddenly felt too tight and itchy, like it was trying to choke me. "I need to get out of these."

Now that I could talk, we needed to talk about what had happened. I just couldn't do it in these clothes, like I was playing dress-up. I needed to do it as me.

Dan followed me up the stairs and peeled off into the master bedroom while I went to the guest room where I'd been staying.

I folded the uniform and brought it back out with me. It should probably be hung up, but I didn't have any hangers.

Dan was already waiting in the hallway. He accepted the uniform and deposited it in his own room.

Each motion we made felt like we were packing time with the tiny, mundane details to delay the inevitable. As if neither of us wanted to talk about what had happened.

Jarrod had finally found me.

I trailed Dan down the stairs and into the kitchen.

He put on a pot of coffee. "This might be a good thing."

"Jarrod showing up is never a good thing." I couldn't keep the bitterness out of my voice.

I didn't deserve the way Jarrod treated me. No one should be abused. No one, no matter what they did, deserved abuse.

But I had picked him. I'd allowed myself to be tricked by him. He'd seemed so charming and sincere at first, and I'd let him rush me into marrying him.

Where was the line between something done to me and personal responsibility? Right or wrong, this feeling that I wouldn't be here if I'd made better choices wouldn't go away.

Dan held out a chair for me, and I sat. "I didn't mean it's a good thing Jarrod is here. I meant maybe it's a good thing he was out in the open. If he was planning to hurt you, wouldn't he have kept his presence a secret? People have seen him now. If anything happens to you, he'll be a suspect."

That would be the case with anyone else. I prayed I was wrong about Jarrod. But I'd lived under his rule for years, and I'd heard all about his job. I'd even gone to parties and listened to others tell me how Jarrod came up with the idea that finally solved the case.

Had he not become an FBI agent with a wife he could secretly unload his rage and control needs on, he might have become an uncatchable serial killer.

I pressed my hands into the top of the table. They shook anyway. "It just means he's come up with a better plan."

One that had him asking questions about Dan.

The coffee maker beeped, and Dan opened the fridge. He grabbed the milk and closed the door. Janie's drawings swayed with the motion.

If Jarrod had found out where Dan lived... "You need to send

Janie away."

Dan stopped, the coffee pot suspended over a mug. When he moved again, his motions were more controlled than before.

He brought two mugs to the table. He set them down, but I didn't reach for mine, and he didn't reach for his. It felt like he was waiting for me to say something more.

"Jarrod was asking about you. He knows now that you lied to him back in May. He knows you knew the name I was using and that I was still in Lakeshore. He knows you were hiding me from him." I met Dan's gaze so that he could see I was calm. This wasn't a panic reaction. I felt the same as I had when I'd finally made the decision to leave Jarrod. I knew that this had to be done. "You're now as much his enemy as I am. You made a fool of him. Whatever he does next, Janie won't be safe here."

What I was asking was a lot. She was in school and Christmas was only a few weeks away.

Dan held my gaze. His expression gave nothing away.

He moved his coffee cup toward him. "I'll send her to her maternal grandparents. My sister-in-law's father was special forces before he retired. Janie will be excited to go visit them, and she'll be safe there."

"Are they out of state?"

Dan nodded. "I'll ask Claire to take her."

That was good. Getting Claire out of town too, if only for a couple of days, was good. If anything happened to either Janie or Claire because of me, I wasn't sure I could live with it.

I moved my coffee mug farther away and lowered my head to the table. Wasn't I supposed to feel safer after I was done testifying at the trial? I was supposed to be safer. No one would want to stop me anymore because I'd already done what they wanted to stop me from doing.

And then Jarrod showed up.

Cold flushed through my body as if I'd stepped outside in January wearing a t-shirt.

We'd thought the cyanide was personal, but we might have been looking in the wrong direction for the person. This might have had nothing to do with the Glover trial.

I lifted my head. "Jarrod might have been behind the cyanide."

Dan took a drink of his coffee as if he were buying himself time to think through what I'd said. "Would he have done that? Rather than waiting to kidnap you."

Jarrod grabbing me was what I'd been worried about from the moment I'd left him. At first, I'd been afraid he'd force me to go back to him. Then I'd been afraid he'd simply kill me and dump my body where it'd never be found.

Now I didn't know what to fear. What would satisfy his pride the most? "I don't know. Poisoning an ingredient would have let him kill me or ruin my career or…"

The next words stuck in my throat. My chest felt tight and too small just thinking about it. Not only because of what I stood to lose but because Dan couldn't help but know how I felt about him once I said it. We'd danced around what would come after I got my divorce. Neither of us had addressed it directly.

But I wanted him to know how important he was to me.

Dan waited, his gaze locked on me, his hands around his mug.

"Or he could have killed you with it," I said. "Killing you would have given him his revenge on you and me at the same time. Dying myself would be more merciful than having to watch you die."

Dan reached his hand out, and I set mine in his.

"I think we have to work under the assumption it was him," he said. "If it was another Tylenol killer, then you're safe. If it was someone targeting the department, then you're safe. If it was someone trying to stop you from testifying, then you're safe. If it was Jarrod, and we think it was one of the others, it puts you at risk."

I'd be at risk anyway with Jarrod in town, but an act like this would prove he was willing to do anything to hurt me. Worse, it meant we couldn't assume anyplace or anyone was safe. We couldn't assume that I was safe because I was surrounded by people. Prior to this, that's what I believed.

Dan gave my hand another squeeze. "We'll work it like we would any other case. Objectively. The way I see it, the first question we need to answer is how he got access to your powdered sugar. If he could get that close to you, why not kill or kidnap you outright?"

9

I knocked on the doorframe of Clare's open door. Her bed looked like she'd laid out enough clothes for a three-week vacation. They couldn't possibly all fit in the wheeled carry-on bag lying on the floor.

"I thought you were only staying for the weekend after you drop Janie off and then coming home."

Claire barely glanced in my direction. "I am." She let out a long sigh as if I should have known why she'd lain out so much of her wardrobe, but that I was being intentionally dense. "The weather there can be unpredictable this time of year, plus I don't know what they set the thermostat in their house at. If they're 76 degree people, I need a t-shirt. If they're 68 degree people, I'll need sweaters."

I probably hadn't given this much thought to my clothes in my whole life. Then again, when I'd been married to Jarrod, he'd told me what to wear. After I left him, I hadn't had enough clothes to make a decision difficult.

You're stalling, Isabel, Fear prodded me gently.

I'd never have expected him to be the one to encourage me to fulfill my promise to talk to Claire. But in a way it made sense. I was scared of what Claire would think if I didn't finally tell her about Mike showing up at the bakery and what he said. By waiting this long, I'd already opened myself up to questions of why I hadn't told her sooner, despite the fact that we'd had a lot going on.

"I was hoping I could talk to you for a minute before you leave."

Claire raised her eyebrows, a tan v-neck t-shirt suspended in the air. She turned her attention back to examining it. "Whatever it is will have to wait. We can't be late checking in for our flight, and I'm already running behind." She extended the shirt toward me. "Does that look like a stain to you?"

Something was up. Claire had to be intentionally avoiding a conversation with me at this point. She could easily talk and pack if she chose to. Although, what I needed to tell her probably would distract her from picking the right clothes for the trip.

"We're here," Dan's voice called from the first floor.

"We're here, we're here, we're here," Janie's voice sang out. "Time to go, Auntie Claire."

The tense lines in Claire's face softened. The title was honorary. Claire was actually Dan's cousin, not his sister. But they acted more like siblings, and Claire played such a huge role in Janie's life that it'd always seemed right.

Claire folded up a few pieces of clothing and put them in her bag. "I suppose I'll have to borrow a cardigan from Louise if I'm too cold. Lord knows that woman has enough of them." Her tone was affectionate rather than scathing. I hadn't asked whether Claire knew Janie's maternal grandparents well or not, but that gave me the answer.

Claire cast a long-suffering look at the remaining clothes on her bed, as if it were their fault and not hers that they'd need to remain out until she returned.

"Do you want me to put them away for you?"

Claire shook her head and scooped up her bag. "I'm trying the Marie Condo method of folding, and it takes practice to get it right."

In other words, I wouldn't save her any time when she returned by putting them away. She'd feel the need to pull them back out and do it again herself.

She went down the stairs, and I trailed after her. She'd handled the news that Janie had to be sent away for safety fairly well, but she'd still been up in the night cleaning again. Having her take Janie was the best choice. She'd at least get a few good night's sleep while she was away. I'd be taking Dan's guest room so that I wouldn't have to stay here alone.

I set my feet on the main floor and a small head connected with my stomach, arms wrapping around me like tentacles.

"I don't understand why you can't come too." My shirt muffled Janie's voice. "Grandma and Grandpa wouldn't mind." She pulled back slightly and looked up at me. "They belong to my first mom like I told you about."

A couple of weeks ago, I'd been babysitting Janie, and we'd been building a Lego house. She'd started talking about her "first dad" and her "first mom," the ones who had to go to heaven early. I hadn't been sure how much she knew about them, but she'd had so many stories that it was quickly clear Dan made a point of telling her about his brother and sister-in-law. Janie had their names memorized, along with their hair and eye color, and the story of her birth in a thunderstorm where the power at the hospital almost went out.

Since then, it was like she'd opened a floodgate, but not of talking about her first mom and first dad. Of making sure I knew that she wanted another mom some day, and she thought it should be me. She'd launched a campaign to let me know what a good daughter she'd be.

That was never in doubt, but it was getting harder and harder to explain to her why it was more complicated than me simply accepting the position and moving into her house permanently.

Dan rested a hand on Janie's head. "We talked about this already. Isabel has things she has to do here that she can't leave."

Not to mention the whole point was to get Janie away from

me, and away from Jarrod, so she'd be safe. Some things you just didn't tell a child.

"Can Isabel come get me when it's time to come home?" Janie asked.

"Maybe." Dan's voice cracked slightly.

We had no idea when Janie would safely be able to come home.

Claire pulled out the handle of her carry-on bag. It made a whoosh-thwap sound. "I'll be waiting out in the car. Don't take too long. Who knows how backed up security will be once we get there."

Dan peeled Janie off me and spun her around toward the door. "You help Claire take her stuff to the car. I'm going to help Isabel with her bags."

"Okay."

The reminder that I was going to stay at their house for a while seemed to give Janie hope that her plan for me moving in permanently was going to succeed. Her grin said it made up for me not going with her. She bunny hopped out of the house.

Dan watched the door close behind them, then motioned for me to lead the way upstairs. "The lab confirmed that none of the sugar from the stores in the city had cyanide in them, and no one else has reported cyanide poisoning. Did you contact Scott about getting the security footage from the shop?"

I'd already filled Scott in on what was happening. I hadn't had much choice considering he was our landlord and the police had temporarily closed our bakery. They would have contacted him had we not.

"He's going to bring them by later today."

Dan gave me the smile that crinkled the corners of his eyes and almost made me forget why I couldn't kiss him yet. "I'll pop popcorn."

Despite the situation, a laugh slipped out of me. Watching hours of dull security footage with anyone else wouldn't have sounded appealing. The idea of sitting on a couch with Dan and talking while we stared at the screen was something I was almost looking forward to.

Besides, it was our only option for trying to figure out when and if Jarrod planted the cyanide in our powdered sugar. We'd been able to narrow the time frame down to something manageable. I'd recently done a restock, and the police hadn't found any cyanide in that. We also knew the cyanide couldn't have been in the powdered sugar long or it would have gotten into the items we'd baked for the shop or one of our custom clients.

We'd been able to narrow it down to the range of a couple of days prior to the murder mystery weekend, also eliminating the times the bakery was staffed. It was still a lot of footage, but less than it could have been. With the bakery closed and Dan on leave from the department, what else did we have to do with our time anyway?

Claire's voice floated up to me, and I stopped halfway up the stairs. I shouldn't have been able to hear her if she was speaking at a normal volume.

That meant she was yelling.

I spun around. Dan was already running back down the stairs toward the door. I sprinted after him.

If Jarrod had showed up, Claire and Janie were in danger.

Dan and I reached the door.

Dan blocked my path with an arm. "If that's Jarrod, you shouldn't go out there." His voice was low but firm.

He was wrong. If that was Jarrod, the people I loved were in danger because of me. "If that's Jarrod, you need to deal with him while I get Janie out of there."

Dan glanced at the door, then nodded. He opened the door enough to assess the situation. For all we knew, Jarrod had a gun on Claire, and we'd need to call 9-1-1 before also putting ourselves in the line of fire.

Dan's shoulders dipped, and then his back stiffened as if the relief of whatever he saw was fleeting. "It's Mike."

His tone carried everything he thought of Claire's ex.

"Are you refusing to date again because you want to keep sucking money out of me for alimony?" With the door open, Mike's raised voice came clearly into the house.

Dan and I both stepped outside.

Janie was in the car, but she'd swiveled around, and her face was pressed to the back window. Her breath fogged up the glass.

Claire stood on the sidewalk just behind the car with her

hands on her hips in her trademark pose. Whatever awful things happened in their marriage, it was clear Claire had at least never suffered physical abuse. Her entire body language screamed *try it, buddy.*

"It's nothing more than you owe me," Claire said. "Who worked to put you through school? You came out without any student debt thanks to me."

I could almost see Mike's eye roll in his body language. "I've repaid that to you twice over in all the sacrifices I've made for you since." He swept an arm in our direction. "Like buying you this house that you still get to live in. The least you could do after everything I've done for you over the years is go on a few dates and try to find another husband."

I'd known Mike's interest in Claire's dating life couldn't be altruistic. He'd just confirmed it. He only cared about Claire in so far as she was costing him money. He wanted to stop having to pay it. It was why he'd delayed divorcing her for so long in the first place even though he'd moved in with his girlfriend, now fiancée.

I leaned closer to Dan. "Should you do something?" I whispered.

He gave the tiniest shake of his head. "She wants me to let her handle things herself."

Claire made a *ha* noise at Mike. "I gave up years of my life catering to you like I was your servant. I don't owe you anything, even if I did have time to date, which I don't."

Mike leaned back on his heels and crossed his arms over his chest. "Too busy with what? Your business isn't even open right now."

If Mike knew about our business being closed, that didn't bode well. News had traveled. We would have a hard time getting all our customers back. Some would never return. We could very well struggle for months thanks to this.

Claire looked like she would have spit venom at him had she had the ability. "Trying to salvage the reputation of our business for one." Claire jerked her head in my direction. "Helping a friend who's also going through a bad divorce for another. Because I know what that's like."

Mike spun and pointed a finger in my direction. I shrank back instinctively.

"You were supposed to help me out by encouraging her to agree when my friend called. Instead, she didn't even give him a chance."

Claire actually laughed this time. "You think I'm stupid enough to date anyone you call a friend. I don't want to be anywhere near a person who'd call you a friend."

Mike's arm tensed in a way that said he'd like to hit Claire, even if he never had before.

Dan must have sensed the shift too. He stepped closer to Mike. "I think it's time for you to leave. If you want to talk to Claire in the future, you can call and make an appointment."

"She won't take my calls." Mike sputtered the words.

"Then that's her choice. Get in your car and go."

Dan-the-loving-father and Dan-the-tender-friend were gone. All that remained was Dan-the-detective, a man who expected to be obeyed.

Mike shot a nasty look in my direction as if I'd betrayed him, then climbed into his car and drove away.

As soon as he was out of sight, Claire slumped against the back bumper of the car. "I know I told you to let me fight my own battles, but I take it back. If he shows up again while you're here, please put him right back in his car and slam the door."

Dan couldn't actually touch Mike or force him to do anything if he wasn't breaking the law. That said, Mike didn't appear to want to cross Dan. In the past, when Claire had finally allowed Dan to intervene, Mike had backed off rather than continuing to push, just like this time.

Some men, no matter what they might say, didn't truly respect women. They always thought men were smarter and knew best. They gave lip service to equality, but their actions said otherwise.

Claire turned a laser-focused glare at me. "What did he mean that you agreed to help him?"

I cringed. I should have known we'd get back to that. "I didn't agree to help him. I agreed to tell you he was getting married. That's what I've been trying to tell you for over a week now."

Something crossed Claire's face that I couldn't interpret. "That's what you were trying to tell me?"

I nodded. "What did you think?"

She put a hand back onto the trunk as if to steady herself. "I wasn't sure. That you wanted out of the business. That you'd decided to leave town after all. That you didn't..."

She glanced back at Janie, who still watched everything through the window. She motioned us away from the car and onto the middle of the lawn.

"I've seen what's going on between the two of you for a while now. I thought maybe with your divorce hearing coming up, it'd brought back a lot of bad memories. Maybe you'd decided you never wanted to marry again."

And that I wanted her help letting Dan down easy.

I peeked Dan's way. His expression had a rare vulnerability to it. It was there and gone, replaced by the calm demeanor I'd come to expect.

He'd always been so careful not to put pressure on me. He'd let me know he was interested, and he'd helped me in every way I needed, but he'd never made me feel like I owed him anything in return.

I hadn't stopped to think about the risk that was for him. How it must have felt to not know if I'd ever be ready to take a step past friendship with him.

"I love our business, and I'm not leaving town. My divorce..." The words stuck in my throat. Even after all this time, revealing what I thought and felt went against every survival instinct I had. But Claire and Dan weren't going to punish me for it or use it against me. "My divorce was a risk I only took so I'd have the freedom to marry again eventually."

Claire gave a sharp nod. Dan slid his hand into mine, a brief squeeze and then gone, reassurance but no pushing. I didn't deserve him. At the same time, I wouldn't have even been able to consider a step like this with anyone who had less patience.

Claire's body language closed in, her shoulders coming forward and her arms tightening against her sides. "When did you talk to Mike?"

Friendships had so many layers that I'd never considered. Claire had been both worried they'd lose me, and angry by my seeming betrayal.

"He stopped by the bakery when Scott and I were closing up shortly before the murder mystery weekend. He wouldn't leave until I promised to tell you."

"And that's what you kept wanting to talk to me about? That's all of it? You're sure?"

I nodded.

Claire sighed. "Next time just blurt it out."

She pivoted on her heel and climbed into the back seat of the car, next to Janie.

I looked sidelong at Dan. "Does that mean I'm forgiven?"

He shrugged. "Hard to tell."

~

WHEN WE GOT BACK FROM DROPPING JANIE AND CLAIRE AT THE airport, Dan cleared his house again, checking room by room. The rooms were empty, and nothing looked out of place.

He hooked his TV up to his laptop, so we could play the surveillance footage Scott sent. Dan popped popcorn on the stove, and I added melted butter and salt when it finished popping. If we had to sit through hours of boring video, I wanted something good to munch on.

Pirate, Janie's cat, must have thought the popcorn smelled good as well because he followed me to the living room and hopped up on the couch beside me. Either that, or he was already missing Janie.

"All set," Dan said.

He sat right next to me on the couch even though there was space on the far side. He looped an arm over my shoulder. The tension in my stomach muscles that I hadn't realized was there until it let go, loosened slightly. Whatever this video showed, I didn't have to face it alone.

Dan clicked the play button. "Let's see if we can catch a killer."

10

*D*an stopped the final video and ached his back into a stretch. "You're sure this is the right time frame? You didn't buy the supplies a day earlier?"

Our days of watching security footage hadn't turned up anything. Jarrod hadn't appeared anywhere on the security footage from the days leading up to the murder mystery weekend. No one with the right build and walk had even appeared in the video. If they had, we could at least entertain the idea he'd disguised himself.

I pulled out my phone and checked my calendar. I kept careful track of when we purchased anything and how much. Not only did it help us remember to restock before we ran out, but Claire used it to help us budget and adjust prices as necessary. "I have the date right."

Dan pulled a leg up on the couch and shifted to face me

rather than continuing to stare at the now-blank TV. "That explains how he got past the security system. He didn't."

He also hadn't sent anyone who broke in during the hours we were closed. Nor had he hired someone to sneak in while we were open. During the hours when we were open, someone would have had to pass by the employee at the counter in order to get to the supplies stored in the back. I'd already asked both Scott and our other employee. Neither of them had seen someone poking around.

"You're sure Abby wouldn't have taken money to let someone into the back?" I asked.

Abby, the high school girl we'd hired, was also Dan and Claire's younger cousin. Technically, she was a second cousin or cousin once removed because she was the daughter of their first cousin. I could never keep the actual designations straight, and their family was so large that no one bothered trying. Everyone was just a *cousin*.

"Maybe she accepted some money and now that—" I stopped myself before saying *now that Zee's dead*. Dan didn't need me constantly reminding him of what he'd lost. "Now with what happened, she might be afraid to come forward. She might think she'll go to prison as an accessory."

She might, though it was unlikely. If she'd allowed someone into our kitchen, it was unethical, but not illegal. She hadn't known the plan was murder.

Dan scratched his forehead slowly. "I can't see it. Abby's a bit infamous in the family for being a stickler for the rules. She doesn't even speed. She doesn't even jaywalk. When she was ten, she shoplifted a chocolate bar because her mom wouldn't buy it for her. Then she took it back the next day and confessed to the store manager what she'd done because she couldn't handle the guilt."

That didn't sound like someone who would so much as bend the rules.

I knew Scott well enough to know he'd never allow anyone into the back either, especially not after what had happened a few months ago with the death of his father. If anyone even showed interest in the back of the shop—let alone tried to get back there—he'd have told me.

Dan turned the TV off, sending the room into dim light, only the moon and the glow from the kitchen illuminating it.

Dan stretched again, and a yawn broke free. "Let's run the timeline one more time before we call it for tonight. When did you make the icing?"

I hadn't made the icing. Dan must not realize that yet. Last time he'd asked me "when did the icing get made?"

"Claire made the icing, not me. We were running a bit behind because the truck didn't want to start in the cold. When we got to the venue, Claire's final prep was quick, so she made the icing and frosted those batches."

Dan straightened, his back coming away from the couch cushion. "She made it at the venue?"

I nodded.

"When did you bring your supplies over?"

Oh no. If he was heading in the direction I suspected he was... "We moved everything we could over the night before."

That had to be why we hadn't seen Jarrod on any of the security footage from our bakery. It also explained why Jarrod hadn't killed me or grabbed me from the store if he had access to it. It also explained why nothing in our store had cyanide in it.

He'd probably gotten into our supplies at the venue, not at the store.

I pressed my fingertips into the space between my eyes. "With people going in and out all day, he would have found it easy to slip into the kitchen there and poison the powdered sugar with cyanide. If he was watching me, he'd have seen us transporting things there. He could have slipped into the kitchen in between our runs."

Dan ran his hands over his face, something he only did when he was exhausted. "That will make it harder for us to link Jarrod to what happened. We'll have to go to the venue and show his picture to the employees. Hopefully one of them will recognize him. Even then, it's not a lock. We can't get him on breaking and entering the way we could if he entered your bakery illegally. If he went to the venue, we only have proximity, not proof."

My stomach felt hot and unhappy. I leaned over my knees, trying to draw in deep breaths. Trying and failing. Jarrod was too smart. He would have planned this all out carefully for months before he acted.

A warm hand rubbed soothing circles in my back.

"Hey." Dan leaned forward slightly so his face was next to mine. "We'll catch him. No one is perfect. Police work is a lot about not giving up until you can collect enough little pieces to break the case open. Okay?"

I nodded. Dan wouldn't give me false hope. He wouldn't say it if it wasn't true. I had to keep reminding myself of that.

Dan stood and stretched again. "We'll talk to everyone at the venue until we find someone who recognizes him. Right now, though, I have to leave, or I'll be late picking Claire up from the airport."

A flicker of a smile tried to move my lips. "No one wants that."

Dan gave a mock shudder. "Definitely not."

He offered a hand. I took it, and he helped me up from the couch.

"Are you sure you wouldn't feel safer coming with me to pick Claire up rather than staying here?"

No doubt I would feel safer. Right now, I didn't want to be alone at all. But things with Jarrod could drag on for a while, and our business had already taken a major blow.

"I'd feel safer, but if I go, I won't finish the cupcakes for Elijah's order in time." Elijah Wells was one of our best regular clients. He ordered a lot of finicky custom work that he paid well for. The longer we worked with him, the more orders he placed. He'd recently become almost a middle man for us, arranging orders for the charities he worked with, even if those order technically had nothing to do with a project he was part of. "Claire's probably going to want to work late tonight making the fillings rather than going to sleep the way she should. Abby's coming tomorrow to help with frosting and decorating."

"Elijah would understand," Dan said.

There'd been a time when he hadn't liked Elijah much. He'd thought Elijah was a murderer who was deceiving me in order to deflect blame from himself. Dan had also been a bit jealous, thinking I'd chosen Elijah over him when I hadn't chosen anyone. I hadn't been able to date because I was married. I was still married, but hopefully not for much longer.

Elijah had become a regular in our life, though, and he and Dan had developed a friendship, despite their differences.

"I'm sure he normally would." I hooked a thumb back toward the kitchen. "But these are for the benefit to raise funds for the clean water initiative. We have tickets, remember? They're on your fridge."

Elijah had arranged for us to also attend the event as guests rather than Claire and I showing up merely to set up the cupcake tower and then leave.

Dan glanced in the direction of the kitchen. "I'd forgotten." He squeezed the hand he was still holding. "Arm the alarm system as soon as I'm gone, and check that all the doors are locked."

"I will."

Dan headed out to his car. I watched through the window as he drove away.

A tight feeling crawled up from my stomach and into my throat. I was alone in the house. I was alone. With Jarrod in the city. And he no doubt knew where Dan lived by now.

Still, how long could I depend on having a babysitter as if I were a child? The threat from Jarrod might stop after the divorce hearing because his secrets would be out. Or it might not. He might want revenge for the way I'd damaged his reputation. Whether or not I was safe would depend on whether he thought he'd be a suspect for my murder if I died after I divorced him.

I scrubbed my hands over my face. The most dangerous time was now, before the divorce hearing. After the hearing, he might find killing me too risky, and he certainly couldn't force me to come back at that point without raising all kinds of suspicions.

I should have gone with Dan to pick up Claire. Better that I stay up late into the night and give up sleep to work on the cupcakes than that I take a risk of staying here alone, even with the alarm set and the doors locked. Jarrod had ways of getting past traditional means of defense.

Dan probably wasn't far away yet.

I pulled out my phone. *I changed my mind. Are you too far away to come back for me?*

My phone let out the whoosh of a sent text. I tucked it back in my pocket, locked the front door, and punched in the code for the alarm.

The screen flashed orange instead of red.

Back door bypassed, the error message said.

Shoot. That was the last thing I needed when I was here alone. Dan's security system wouldn't arm a door or a window if the sensors indicated it wasn't closed. He'd gone a whole week last month with one window that wouldn't arm because the sensor kept malfunctioning. Hopefully this time we simply hadn't shut the back door securely enough.

If it was a problem with the sensor, Dan could call the security company tomorrow, but that didn't help me tonight. Texting him had definitely been the right idea.

Assuming he read it before he reached the airport. Dan didn't text and drive, so he'd have to pull off to check his text.

First, I'd check the back door to make sure it was shut tight, and then I'd call Dan instead. He always had Bluetooth enabled.

I headed through the kitchen and straight to the back door. I gave it a push. It clicked into place.

The problem wasn't with the sensor. That was a relief.

Except this door couldn't have been left open by Janie, which was what usually caused a bypass error. The alarm system armed normally last night. I'd gone out into the backyard this morning to stretch my legs, but I was sure I'd shut it carefully. I always worried that if I didn't, Pirate would escape.

The prickly feeling of hairs standing up on my neck and arms covered my body.

I needed to set the alarm on the house. Then if Jarrod were inside, I could set off the alarm as long as I could reach a door or window.

Or I should get out of here. But where would I go? Would it be safer to sit in Claire's car? Or drive her car somewhere public and call Dan on the way?

Somewhere with people would definitely be safer.

My purse with the keys was by the front door, along with my shoes.

I turned.

Jarrod stood blocking my path back to the living room. "Finally we get to talk privately."

My arms and legs felt too heavy to move, and a rushing sound filled my ears.

He pushed himself off the wall where he'd been leaning. "Amy, darlin', come here and let me see you."

My legs moved in response to his command. Like I was a robot, and he held my remote control.

I stopped in front of him. This was a bad dream. It had to be a bad dream. I'd had nightmares about Jarrod finding me a hundred times before. In a minute, I'd wake up on the couch beside Dan, and he'd tease me about falling asleep and leaving him to watch the boring surveillance videos alone.

Jarrod slid a hand around my waist. He pulled me closer and kissed me softly.

Bile burned my throat. I swallowed it down. I knew what would happen if I threw up on him.

"Hasn't this gone on long enough, darlin'?"

His hand moved up and down my side in a way that used to send pleasant tingles through my body when we were dating. Now my skin shivered like it was trying to crawl off my body to escape.

There wasn't any escape.

He turned us around so that my back was to the wall, and he kissed me again. "I've missed you. It's time to come home. We'll forget about all of this and start over."

My mind retreated somewhere deep where I could barely feel his hand on my waist anymore.

His suggestion wasn't a choice. It was never a choice. He was telling me what I'd do, and I'd have to do it or suffer the consequences.

"If you still want to bake, you can bake cupcakes for me to take into the office." The tone of his voice was magnanimous, like he was offering me a prize, and it made him a good husband to let me keep my hobby. "I know everyone will love your baking. I always did. I used to tell everyone how talented you were."

He probably had. He'd made sure that on the outside we looked like a devoted couple in love. He made sure people knew I was shy and uncomfortable in social situations as a way of explaining away anything odd about my behavior. He made sure to praise me in public so no one would suspect what he did in private.

A tear escaped before I could stop it. I couldn't live like that again. But if I didn't go with him, he'd kill me. I didn't want to die, either.

Jarrod wiped the tear away before it could drip off my chin. "No need to cry, darlin'. I know it's been hard for you on your own, and people have manipulated you into doing things you wouldn't have wanted to do. But that's over now. I'm here, and I'm going to take care of you again, just like always. Whatever misunderstandings we've had are all in the past."

Misunderstandings.

That was what he called it when I'd do something to make him angry, and he'd beat me. The next day he'd apologize for our *misunderstanding*. Or he'd forgive me for making him so angry. Either way, it was always my fault in the end.

I knew better now. It was never my fault. Nothing I did merited the way he hurt me.

The alarm system beeped and then shut off.

"Isabel," Dan's voice called.

Jarrod yanked me close. "Time to go. We don't need him confusing you."

My mind cleared, and I could feel Jarrod's painful grip on my wrist. I could feel how the kitchen was slightly cold from the door being ajar before I'd closed it.

I didn't want to die, but I would rather die than go back.

Jarrod hauled me toward the door.

I yanked away, making my body dead weight against his hold.

"Dan!" I screamed so loud my throat burned. "Help!"

Jarrod spun us around so that his chest pressed into my back, and my body acted as a shield between him and whatever came.

Dan burst through the door, his gun drawn. He slid to a stop. "Let her go, and slowly raise your hands."

"You don't want to do this, Detective. You have a family and career to think of." Jarrod's voice had taken on the tone that I was sure he used at work when talking down hostile suspects. "Your obsession with my wife has gone on long enough, but she doesn't want to stay here anymore. If you let us go now, I won't report you for drawing a gun on a fellow officer."

Dan's expression remained stony except for a slight raise of his eyebrows. "A fellow officer who committed a crime. You invaded my home."

"My wife invited me in. She wanted to reconcile. Apparently you pressured her into filing for divorce."

The tiniest flicker of doubt passed over Dan's face as if he wasn't sure. I was an abuse survivor. And he had wanted me to divorce Jarrod. He could think that maybe I had given in only because he wanted it. That everything between us had happened because I didn't feel like I could say no.

Jarrod wouldn't let me give a long speech to convince Dan otherwise. I might be able to get one short thing out. I could think of only one thing to say that would let Dan know the truth. "Please don't let him."

The same words I'd said the last time we'd encountered Jarrod. They summed up everything. Please don't let him trick you. Please don't let him take me.

Whatever doubt had been playing across Dan's features vanished. His grip tightened on his weapon. "Come to me, Isabel. He's going to let you go."

"Amy," Jarrod put emphasis on my name, "is a vulnerable person and easily taken advantage of. I've already petitioned the court to have her deemed incompetent so that I can take care of her. It should go through any day now."

Dear God, please no, was all I could think.

If he somehow succeeded, I'd be his forever. No one would believe anything I said. Nothing Dan could do or say would be able to free me.

Dan's mouth lifted on one side. If he was scared or concerned at all, it didn't show. He'd stepped into the role he must have used when working undercover. All confidence. "I can call a bluff when I see one. Isabel hasn't been examined by any doctor qualified to make that assessment, and no doctor who examines her will testify that she's mentally incompetent."

Jarrod's body didn't tense or even twitch. "Everyone has secrets they don't want revealed. It's the FBI's job to search them out."

His grip on my wrist felt like it was burning my skin. *Everyone has secrets,* he'd said. He'd found out something about one of the doctors who could deem someone mentally incapable, and he'd used it to make sure he'd win his suit.

Jarrod moved us backward toward the door. "Last chance to let us leave, Detective. I'd rather not have to ruin what has otherwise been a decorated career as far as I can tell."

"This is your last chance, too." Dan's voice was hard in a way that I'd never heard before. "If you move one more step toward that door, I will shoot you."

"If anything happens to me, it'll be your word against mine."

"It'll be Isabel's word as well."

I could almost feel Jarrod smirk. "Again, she's not in her right mind. If anything happens to me, the police will find all the evidence they need to put you in prison for it and to lock Isabel up in an institution."

It wasn't a bluff. I knew what Jarrod sounded like when he bluffed. Whatever he'd fabricated, it would implicate Dan and call my capabilities into question.

Jarrod released his hold on my waist. "So what's going to happen is that I'm going to leave now. I'll see Amy later once the paperwork comes through."

Dan didn't lower his gun.

"Let him go." The words rasped out of my throat.

Dan shook his head.

I took a step toward Dan, and Jarrod didn't stop me. "I'm staying here, and he's going to go."

Before Dan could do anything about it, Jarrod slipped out the door.

Dan darted past me, locked the door, and armed the system. He shoved his gun into its holster and spun around. "What are you doing? He broke in here and tried to kidnap you." He pulled out his cell phone. "We're going to report this immediately."

I placed a hand on his phone. "I know Jarrod better than you do. He's one step ahead of us, and whatever he's put together would have ruined us both had you shot him, whether he lived or died from the wound."

Dan's thumb hovered over the keypad. "We can lock him up right now and this will be over."

"He'll say I let him in. Because of what he's already put in place, they won't be able to prove otherwise. Then if we try to show he murdered Zee by poisoning my sugar, it'll look like we're on a vendetta. No one will listen to us. I had to buy us time." I eased his phone down, and he let me do it. "I need you to trust me. The only way we win is if we out-think him. It's how I got away. I knew he was convinced I was as anti-religion as he was, so I went to church for help."

Dan slid his phone into his pocket, but his motions were

halting, as if he still wasn't sure it was the right thing to do. "What do you have in mind?"

I'd let Jarrod control me for too long. I'd spent all this time on the defensive. This time, we'd be on the offense. I was making my own choices from now on. I trusted Dan. I had to trust myself, too. "First, we find multiple independent doctors and have assessments done that show I'm perfectly capable of taking care of myself and making my own decisions." I put my shoulders back and lifted my chin. "Then we prove that he put cyanide in my powdered sugar and killed Zee. He doesn't know we suspect him, so he's not protecting himself. He'll go to prison, and we won't ever have to worry about him again."

11

"We might have to contact your friend Nicole again." Dan held the door open for me to the hotel that hosted the murder mystery weekend. "Maybe her husband can recommend some doctors he trusts who do competency exams."

I brushed the light dusting of snow off my jacket. Snow was beautiful, no doubt, but I hated the way it melted on my clothes and gave them a musty wet smell. Snow was one part of northern living I could do without. "Once we're done here, I can try calling her on your phone."

I still wasn't going to use mine. There was no way I was going to risk Jarrod going after Nicole and her family, especially not now.

Besides, it was a long shot that her husband would be able to recommend a doctor for what we needed. He was a medical examiner, not a practicing M.D. His colleagues all dealt with dead people.

That said, it was our best option. The doctors Jarrod bribed to say I wasn't capable of caring for myself were probably back in Florida, but we couldn't be sure. The last thing we needed was to hire a doctor to assess me who was really a double agent. If Nicole's husband could at least give us the name of someone he trusted, we'd be less likely to accidentally hire someone who would turn on me at the last minute.

I loosened my scarf. Jarrod still felt like he had a massive lead on us with how quickly our divorce hearing was approaching. But I wasn't giving up. I hadn't come this far to let him win.

"Detective Holmes." A middle-aged woman wearing a bun and dressed in the hotel's black and white uniform called out from behind the front desk. She said something quietly to the other desk clerk and came around to meet us. "I'd say it's a pleasure to have you back but..."

She shrugged as if to say *can you blame me when your party ended up with a dead body?* Her name tag read *Cindy* and below that *Manager.*

Dan pulled out a picture of Jarrod. I hadn't asked him how he got it. Jarrod didn't have any social media accounts because of his job, and I hadn't brought any pictures of him with me when I fled. Dan would have had to use something he had access to due to his position on the police force. Since he wasn't on this case and had probably accessed a system he shouldn't unofficially access, I figured I was better off not knowing. I couldn't get him in trouble if I didn't know anything.

"We need to show this picture to your employees," Dan said, "and see if any of them noticed this man hanging around before our event."

Cindy unbuttoned and rebuttoned her jacket. "I've already had three employees call out sick, and I'm sure it was either stress-related or they're too frightened to come to work. Is this really necessary? We've answered all the questions the other detectives asked."

I would have started wheedling and begging to try to get her to help. Instead, I bit the inside of my cheek and stayed quiet.

Dan stayed so still and calm he could have been a statue, despite having no legal grounds to be here asking questions. At times like this, I could see why he'd made such a great under-cover cop.

"It's necessary," he said. "We think this man might have had something to do with the murder. If we can place him here prior to the crime, we'll be one step closer to putting him away. Which should make your employees feel much safer in the end."

Cindy cocked her head to one side, as if she were weighing his arguments. She held out her hand. "Show it to me again, please."

Dan handed the photo to her.

She stared down at it, then slowly shook her head. "I was

working closely with your department that day, and I don't remember seeing him."

"What about around the kitchen area, rather than the ballroom."

She shook her head. "Kitchen, ballroom, anywhere. The only people going in and out were police officers, her,"—she nodded at me—"and another woman who looked like she was in her sixties. Slender."

That sounded like Claire.

Dan pulled his phone from his pocket, as if he'd had the same thought. He swiped through it, then turned it to face Cindy. "This woman."

"That's her."

Dan slid his phone back into his pocket. "I'll still need to speak to any employee who was on duty the day before and the morning of the event."

Cindy let out a long-suffering sigh. "I think they're all here today. I'll set you up in one of our conference rooms."

She pivoted on her heel and motioned for us to follow her. As she did, I was sure I heard her mumbled something about never renting out space to the police again.

When she'd agreed to host the event, she'd probably thought this would be an easy one. They were the police after all. They shouldn't damage anything or cause any kind of trouble that another group would. Instead, she'd ended up with a murder, her staff being pulled away from their work more than once to answer questions, and bad press. None of those things were what a manager wanted to have to report to their superiors.

She led us into a conference room and turned to go.

"I'm sorry," I said before she could disappear down the hallway. "For all the trouble this has caused you."

"It's not your fault." She powerwalked down the hallway before I could decide whether she meant it or not.

In a way, it was my fault. Jarrod came here and hurt people because of me. If I'd moved on from Lakeshore long ago the way I'd planned to, Zee would still be alive.

I peeked at Dan out of the corner of his eye. He had to have had the same thoughts. Maybe he was even second guessing his decision to convince me to stay and wishing he'd let me leave so that his best friend would still be alive.

"I can see on your face that you don't believe her." Dan's words were soft even though we were alone in the room. "Jarrod made his own choices. He chose to hurt people. You didn't force him to do anything. He chose."

He chose.

The words struck into my core, and something inside felt like it split. I'd told myself so many times since I fled that nothing I'd done had merited the way Jarrod beat me. But none of my self-assurances had sunk in deep enough.

Today they felt true for the first time. One of the few things we truly had control over in life was our reactions. We couldn't even control our emotions, but we could control the way they made us act and what we did about them. Even if I'd screamed at Jarrod, which I hadn't, or if I'd broken things that belonged to him, which I also hadn't, it wouldn't have made it right for him to hit me. Nothing I said or did made it right.

I was not responsible for Jarrod's actions or his crimes. He chose his path, and hopefully he'd soon have to suffer the consequences.

I pulled my chair closed to the table and straightened my spine. "You're right. I'm not to blame for this."

And for the first time, I believed it.

HOURS LATER, WE CLIMBED BACK INTO DAN'S CAR NO FURTHER ahead. None of the employees remembered seeing anyone who looked like Jarrod in the time frame between when Claire and I started bringing in our supplies and when Zee died.

The only people they'd seen around the ballroom and kitchen were police officers and Claire and I.

I clicked my seatbelt into place. If we couldn't show that Jarrod was here, it might not be possible to prove he'd been behind Zee's death. But he had to have been there. The hotel was the only opening for him to poison our sugar.

I'd read an article once that detailed a research study that had tested how well people remembered the faces of those in uniform or in official positions. One of the tests had involved switching the employee at a hotel check-in desk while the person checking in was looking the other way. Very few people realized a change had taken place even when it was significant—for example, from a brown-haired desk clerk wearing glasses to a blond desk clerk without them. Perhaps the hotel employees didn't remember seeing Jarrod because he'd been in a uniform like all the other officers who were setting up.

"Do you think the staff might have overlooked him if he was in a police uniform?"

Dan checked his blind spot before pulling the car out of the parking spot. "That's possible for the hotel staff, but the actual officers would have noticed someone who wasn't one of them, especially if that person was wearing a uniform."

That was true. A stranger dressed in a uniform would have immediately drawn the attention of multiple officers. Which was too bad in a way. If Jarrod had somehow stolen a uniform, it would have given us another avenue to try to pin this on him. He would have had to steal that uniform, and that would have been reported.

"Can you check into whether a uniform has gone missing in the past few weeks just in case?"

"I'll try, but..."

But he wasn't supposed to be investigating this case. He wasn't supposed to be investigating any case right now. He'd been given a short leave to grieve.

His fingers drummed on the steering wheel. "We're not done

yet. Jarrod bribed or blackmailed doctors to falsify medical assessments of you. He might have also bribed or blackmailed an employee to plant the cyanide."

That added a risk to Jarrod's plan in that there would be someone who could identify him and break under pressure if caught. But Jarrod had probably thought about ways to deal with that, maybe even planning to kill the employee later and frame it as a suicide. Having an employee put the poison in my sugar did make more sense than Jarrod trying to sneak in around a group of police officers.

"I'll see if the detectives on the case are open to the suggestion," Dan said. "They seemed like reasonable enough guys. They just don't want any of us actively involved."

I heard the risk there, even if Dan didn't want to worry me by saying it. He had been actively involved. Suggesting an employee might have been forced into conspiracy to commit murder by my abusive husband would result in the detectives on the case re-interviewing the employees. One of them might mention that Dan had already talked to them.

We didn't have many other choices though.

Dan nodded at his phone. "Why don't you call Nicole while we're driving?"

We did need to make use of every minute we had if we were going to stop Jarrod's plans. I picked up Dan's phone and dialed Nicole's number. The call routed through the Bluetooth in Dan's car.

"This is Nikki." Her voice was slightly crackly, which could have been because she was going through the car speakers or it could have been because the town where she lived was notorious for its poor cell phone reception.

So much had changed since we'd last seen each other, including how she answered the phone, but hearing her voice still gave me the sense of reuniting with a long-time friend. Which was unusual in one way. We hadn't been in the same town long, and we'd barely been able to talk since, but she'd been my first friend after I left Jarrod. She was the first time I felt like I could trust someone other than myself. In a lot of ways, she'd paved the way for the friendships I now had.

"It's Isabel. I need your help again."

I filled her in on everything that had happened and what I was looking for.

Nicole let out a long breath of air. "I feel responsible. I'm the one who convinced you that it was important to fight for people who couldn't fight for themselves."

She didn't need to feel guilty for that any more than I needed to feel guilty for the things Jarrod had done. "I made my choice, and I don't regret it."

"When this is all over, then, I hope you'll finally come visit. Hang on. My arm is falling asleep." Her end of the line filled with soft shuffling noises and the rustling of blankets. "I don't know if Mark will be able to help, but Chief McTavish has a contact in the FBI. He could investigate the doctors who've signed the documents declaring you incompetent."

"No!" The word shot out of me loud and forceful, before I could stop it. I intentionally lowered my voice. "Sorry. No. Jarrod is FBI. We can't trust anyone in the FBI."

There was silence on Nicole's end, as if she were carefully considering my words. "Chief McTavish is as honest as it gets. He came here to investigate because the previous chief was corrupt, and he did his job, regardless of how he felt about anyone in the department. I think that if he says we can trust this agent, we can trust him. If you want, I can make sure this agent hasn't ever worked in Florida. Would that help?"

Jarrod had been stationed a few other places as well. "Florida, Arizona, or Texas."

"Okay." She didn't even hesitate. No matter whether she agreed that it was necessary, it was important to me, so she was willing to adjust. "If he hasn't worked in any of those places, can we see if he'll look into it?"

I glanced at Dan. He nodded. He thought Nicole's idea was a good one.

Alongside Claire, they were the people I trusted most in the world. "Yes."

"It's still a longshot." Nicole's voice was soothing, like she knew her news was bad, and she wanted to soften the blow as much as possible. "We'll have to prove not only that these doctors have been bribed or blackmailed, but also connect them to Jarrod. It could take time."

Time was one of the things we had in short supply. "Anything could help."

Nicole was a lawyer. I didn't have to explain the stakes to her. She knew as well as I did what it would mean if I was declared mentally incapable of caring for myself and Jarrod was made my guardian.

"I'll ask Mark if there are any doctors he can personally vouch for who could assess you as well. It's not really his field, though. And I don't think secondhand recommendations are good enough in this situation."

They weren't. Unless Mark was confident in the doctors' character, they could be bought by Jarrod and turned against me. "Thanks again."

"Always. That's what friends are for."

12

I'd barely disconnected the call with Nicole when the phone rang again.

Dan tapped the button on his steering wheel that allowed him to answer. "Holmes."

"It's Miranda. Are you alone?"

Detective Austen's voice had an anxious edge to it. I could imagine her pacing the floor on her end of the call.

She was on leave the same as Dan, but based on her determination to stay in the loop on this case, she probably wasn't actually staying away from the station. Maybe she'd found out something, either from the investigating detectives or because she was secretly investigating as well. She and Dan were supposed to go to the shooting range together tomorrow, so whatever she'd found out must be urgent if she hadn't wanted to wait even one day.

Dan held a finger to his lips, indicating I should stay quiet. "I'm driving in my car."

Answering a question without either lying or telling the truth had probably been a skill that had served him well as an undercover officer.

"I was down at the station again, and the same man showed up. The one who said he was an FBI agent."

My neck and back felt stiff, as if I'd laid down in cement. That couldn't be good. Jarrod already knew where Dan lived. He didn't need to dig up that information anymore.

"He is an FBI agent," was all Dan said.

"I know." Her voice sounded even more agitated. "Labreck was the one who listened to his complaint, and he wasn't as careful about kicking me out as the detectives sent in for Zee's case."

Her voice broke slightly on Zee's name, but she finished the sentence. I'd never liked Detective Austen, but seeing her struggle like this made me pity her. Zee had been Dan's friend, but he'd been Detective Austen's boyfriend. She might have been imagining a life with him, maybe even marriage and kids. Now her days were never going to look the same.

I gave myself a little shake. Proving our theory that Jarrod killed Zee would give her closure, too. I had to stay focused on what trick Jarrod might be up to in order to stop us.

"Dan," Detective Austen's voice slowed in tempo, as if she wanted to be sure she took him seriously, "what's going on?"

That question was vague enough that, short of telling her everything, Dan couldn't answer. And we were definitely not going to tell her everything. Dan wasn't supposed to be investigating this case. The detectives in charge might overlook Detective Austen showing up at the station every day because it was something a lot of grieving family members did in the pursuit of answers and closure. But what Dan and I were doing could be considered actively interfering with the case. Dan had interviewed potential witnesses, after all.

Dan cast me a look that said *don't worry*. "What do you mean?"

"He wanted to file an attempted assault charge against you. He said you drew your weapon on him and threatened him."

I sucked in a breath, then covered my mouth with my hand. Hopefully Detective Austen hadn't heard it.

Jarrod had gone to the police anyway. I should have known he wouldn't wait. Dan was an obstacle standing in his way. He was going to take him out.

I should have let Dan shoot him when we had the chance. Jarrod was never going to stop unless he was dead or in prison.

The seatbelt felt tight and restrictive. I wanted to move, but I couldn't open the door without giving away my presence and missing the rest of the conversation.

Dan removed his hands from the steering wheel and rested them next to him. "Technically that's true."

Detective Austen let out a whoosh of air. "A single mistake

can follow you everywhere if you're not careful. I think you still have time to fix this. It sounded like he would accept a formal apology if you confessed and set up a meeting at the station. Everyone knows you're upset about Zee's...about Zee too and you're not thinking straight. Internal Affairs will probably mandate anger management classes, but it's better than losing your badge over one error in judgment."

A single mistake. An error in judgment. Whatever story Jarrod told had been convincing. From the sounds of it, Detective Austen had hung around to eavesdrop on it and then had immediately called Dan to try to protect him from himself.

That last part of me that was holding her treatment of me during Bob Jenner's murder investigation against her softened. She'd been hard on me because, in her eyes, I was a potential suspect, and someone who necessitated her to bend the rules. I'd also been meddling in the case. But she had Dan's back as a fellow officer, and that was more important.

"It's not what he made it sound like," Dan was saying.

"He made it sound like you were jealous of him trying to reconcile with his wife. You walked in on them in the middle of that reconciliation and went into a rage."

She emphasized the word *reconciliation*. I bent over my knees and covered my face. What she really meant, the story Jarrod was telling everyone, was that Dan had walked in on Jarrod and I in bed together.

"There was no *reconciliation* going on." Dan's voice had

taken on an edge that I hadn't heard before. The way he emphasized the same word gave it an entirely different meaning. "His wife has been living under an assumed name out of fear for her life. What I interrupted was a kidnapping attempt."

Detective Austen sucked in a breath. "It'll be your word against his. He claims you've got some sort of Stockholm thing going on with his wife, and that she's too frightened to say anything against you."

"Did Labreck believe him?" Dan asked.

"I don't know. He told Special Agent Miller that he'd bring you in for questioning." There was a pause where I could almost see her shaking her head. "He's FBI, Dan."

He's FBI. It was why I'd waited so long to run, and why I was sure for the longest time that no one would believe me. Even though Dan was also a police officer, the FBI carried more respect and weight. And Jarrod was an even better actor than Dan must have been in his undercover work.

"Domestic violence calls are the most dangerous for a reason," Detective Austen said. "You need to be careful."

"I will. Thanks for letting me know."

They disconnected the call.

I slowly straightened in my seat. "I should have..." I shook he head. I didn't know how to finish that sentence. "Why didn't you tell Detective Austen that we think Jarrod might be behind the cyanide?"

Dan turned on the car. "We don't have any evidence. If I

accuse him of anything now without proof, it'll make me seem guilty and him innocent, not the other way around. Since I don't know how many allies we'll have once Jarrod finishes, I didn't want to risk losing the one we do have."

That made sense. Detective Austen had the wrong version of the story, but she'd called Dan to hear him out. And to warn him.

Dan glanced in my direction. "Are you up to speaking to Detective Labreck right now?"

I focused on the direction we were headed. Dan had started us off toward the police station rather than back to his house.

"You're going to whether I do or not?" It was more of a statement than a question. I could tell he was.

"Going in voluntarily is the only way to potentially defuse this."

"We should have reported it last night the way you wanted to."

I'd talked him out of it. I'd thought we should lull Jarrod into a false sense of security. If we reported him, I figured he'd bring out all the false accusations against Dan. He'd deny everything, and there was no way we could prove it. He was an FBI agent after all.

I'd played things wrong.

"We'll tell Labreck the truth," Dan said. "It took me until today to convince you that we needed to report it. It's not uncommon for victims to be afraid of reporting their abusers. He'll understand that."

He might understand that, but that didn't mean he'd believe us. The damage to Dan's reputation might already be done.

13

"*I*'d say it's good to see you again, Ms. Miller," Detective Labreck lowered himself into a chair in a way that made him seem exhausted, "but under the circumstances..."

Under the circumstances, he was now in a terrible position. One of his colleagues was accused of things that would cost his job.

All my mind could focus on was that he'd called me *Ms. Miller*, as if I were here on Jarrod's behalf. "I'd prefer if you'd call me Isabel." That couldn't be taken as lying about my name, could it? I'd had to avoid that for so long. I didn't want to accidentally do it now. "My legal name is Amy Miller, but I prefer Isabel."

Detective Labreck looked at me without saying anything. Given how long I'd been waiting, he must have already spoken to Dan. He slowly nodded. "Why don't you tell me what happened on the night in question."

I started from Dan leaving to pick Claire up at the airport and ended when Jarrod finally left.

Detective Labrek's stare felt like he was x-raying me, looking for a hidden break in my story.

"I'm going to be off this case soon, Ms. Mil—Isabel. Internal Affairs will be here tomorrow. So I need you to be completely straight with me. Did you invite your husband over?"

I could say so much in response to that. I could describe the way I'd been hiding from Jarrod for two years. I could tell him about the panic attacks I got when I saw him or even thought he could be nearby.

But all of that would have been over-explaining and could sound like I was trying too hard. In this case, the simplest, most honest answer seemed like the best. "Absolutely not."

Labreck scooted his chair closer to the table. "I might believe you, but IA is going to say it's too convenient. Your husband just happened to pick the one moment when you were alone, right before you set the alarm system, to enter the house."

I wasn't stupid. I hadn't spent years listening to Jarrod tell stories about his interrogations—stories he probably shouldn't have shared with me—not to recognize that Detective Labrek was trying to make me feel like we were on the same team against Internal Affairs.

And maybe we were. Maybe he believed Dan and me. He

could be trying to prep us, even warn us about what was coming once Internal Affairs was the one conducting the investigation. Or maybe he was hoping that if I felt like he was helping me, I'd slip up.

"It wasn't convenient. It also wasn't because I orchestrated the timing. He got into the house at the perfect moment because he'd probably been watching us all day, waiting for that moment."

I kept my tone confident but not angry.

"I'm going to level with you, Isabel."

The use of my chosen name suddenly grated on me as well. It felt like he was using it to try to build a relationship between us where there wasn't one, hoping I'd let down my guard enough to make a mistake.

He leaned forward slightly. "I believe that Dan believes the story you've given him. I believe that whatever he did, he felt he had to do to protect you. What I'm not sure about is you. Are you playing both men against each other, inviting one over and then pretending you didn't want him there when the other shows up?"

My head felt hot, the way it did when I was going to be sick. This was what Jarrod meant when he said no one would believe me. Whatever circumstance I found myself in, his reputation would always clear him of blame. Detective Labrek thought Dan was somehow innocent, but he wasn't sure I was. Because Dan and Jarrod were cops, and I was nobody.

I hadn't filed any police reports. I had no evidence that Jarrod had done the things I said he'd done.

Almost no evidence.

When my lawyer, Mr. Kirkland, took on my divorce case, he'd wanted corroborating evidence too. He'd said the courts would grant my divorce regardless, but it'd go easier if I had some proof.

"Dan is my best friend, the person I love most in the world." The words didn't stick coming out the way I'd expected them to. "My husband—"

My voice gave out. Calling him that made me feel trapped. I could be trapped if he succeeded in having me declared incompetent.

"Jarrod abused me in every sense of the word, beginning shortly after we were married until I left him. There's a pastor and his wife at a little church where I used to live who will vouch for me, as will the woman who runs the women's shelter where the pastor's wife took me. My lawyer also has x-rays on file from a doctor here in Lakeshore who examined me. They'll show you evidence of old breaks that weren't properly set. All of it will be on record in a few days once my divorce hearing takes place. So please do check out my story. But do it fast because if you're looking at me, you're not looking at Jarrod. And that's the person who needs to be stopped."

My chest felt lighter as soon as the words were out. That had to be the longest speech I'd ever given to a police officer. I was done letting Jarrod silence me with the fear that I wouldn't be believed. The truth was the truth whether anyone believed me or not, and I'd continue to speak it.

Detective Labreck gaze hadn't moved from my face during my whole speech, but now his eyes shifted back and forth as if he were processing what I'd said. "Let's say I believe you. For argument's sake. When IA gets here, you're going to need to have a good reason why you didn't report the home invasion and attempted kidnapping immediately."

Everything looked clear in hindsight. Maybe this would all be over if I hadn't convinced Dan that was a bad idea. Then again, Jarrod was smart. He'd planned for that contingency too. "Jarrod said he'd created files full of false evidence against Dan. He threatened to use them. And he's trying to have me deemed mentally incompetent so that I'll be under his control permanently. I thought that..."

I was rambling again. I could feel it. And I didn't know exactly what I'd thought. Not coming directly to the police seemed foolish and naïve now. It all came down to one thing. "He told me for years that if I ever told anyone what he was doing, no one would believe me. I thought no one would believe me. I thought the truth wouldn't be enough."

I made a point of meeting Detective Labreck's gaze. To his credit, he looked away.

I leaned forward slightly. If this was my only chance for someone to listen, I was going to say it all. "We wanted to get proof of the other things we think he's done before we accused him of anything. With a man like Jarrod, you don't get second chances."

Detective Labrek's gaze came back to my face. His eyes were tense around the edges. "And what do you think he's done?"

"Poisoned Zee Garcia with cyanide."

He drooped in his seat, all his hard lines turning into soft angles. The detective was gone and a normal man sat in front of me.

"That's what Dan said too. I was hoping he was wrong. Those outsiders the powers-that-be brought in aren't looking in remotely the right direction."

"Dan told you our theory?"

Labreck glanced over his shoulder, as if he didn't want to risk someone walking in on us. "He can't go to the team assigned to this case. Not now. But I still can." He tugged on the edges of his collar, opening it up slightly. "I'll be out of the game after IA arrives, but I'll do everything I can to help you until then, even if I have to risk my job and look into the hotel employees myself."

"I still think you should have asked for alimony and half his property." Claire leaned forward from the back seat of the car. "After everything he put you through, it's the least he could do."

I laced and unlaced my fingers on my lap as Dan pulled the car into a parking spot at the courthouse. Alimony and half of everything is exactly what Claire had demanded once Mike finally stopped blocking their divorce in every possible way he could. Her requests ended up holding up their divorce further as Mike countered. In the end, though, the judge had awarded Claire what she asked for.

And now she had to deal with Mike trying to weasel his way out of alimony payments every month. "Alimony would mean I'd have to have contact with Jarrod every month, even if only through his name on a check. And I'm leaving the marriage with what I came in with. I don't want anything of his."

Claire sniffed. "He prevented you from working. That should cost him something."

She was only trying to help. I knew that. But she didn't fully understand. She and Mike had been happy once, even if his true nature had come through the longer their marriage went on. Had he not cheated on her and then moved out to be with his girlfriend, she'd still be married to him. Claire looked back on her life and saw how she spent it supporting what Mike wanted, only to have him abandon her once they should have been enjoying the results of all their hard work together. For her, it made sense to want part of what she'd worked so hard for.

I didn't want repayment. All I wanted was my freedom. I wanted to be able to use my real name, to be able to legally change my name. I wanted to work and date and live, all without looking over my shoulder.

Divorcing Jarrod wouldn't give me all those things, but it'd be a very important step.

Mr. and Mrs. Kirkland, my lawyer and his wife, stood in the overhang of the courthouse door, out of the falling snow. Mrs. Kirkland didn't normally attend her husband's court appearances, she'd told me, but she wanted to be here today. She was the reason I'd hired her husband for this.

Both Nicole and Eve had offered to come as well. I'd turned Nicole down because she shouldn't be traveling with a baby in tow in December, and I turned Eve down because I didn't know what awful things Jarrod would say. Eve had been in a different kind of abusive relationship. It didn't seem fair to ask her to be somewhere that might bring back difficult memories for her memories.

Assuming everything went well, though, Eve was taking me out to a celebratory lunch tomorrow.

Nicole had texted me multiple Bible verses all morning about God being in control and that I didn't need to worry.

We got out of the car. Mrs. Kirkland scurried out into the snow and looped her arm through mine. "Today's the big day, sweetie. Are you excited?"

I wouldn't have said excited. She probably didn't ask most people getting a divorce if they were excited, but she knew my story. "More like I'm afraid I might throw up all over my shoes."

Mrs. Kirkland squeezed my arm. "That's normal. It's a big life change."

Mr. Kirkland held the door open for all of us, and we headed inside.

The room we entered wasn't a courtroom like I'd testified in during the Glover trial. It was much smaller, with no jury box and limited seating. If many more people had come to support me, we'd have had to fill up Jarrod's side of the room.

I forced myself to walk to my spot behind one of the two tables without looking in Jarrod's direction. If I looked his way, I might not make it there.

Mr. Kirkland held out my chair for me, and I sank into it. I could do this. I had to do this. I would do this.

After this, if Jarrod threatened me in any way, I'd get a restraining order. And if he didn't go to prison for Zee's murder, I'd make sure to enforce that restraining order if Jarrod so much as violated the distance in the order by an inch.

I turned my head in the direction of his table.

His lawyer sat there alone. The man wore a suit that looked more expensive than the clothes my side of the room was wearing combined. He tapped a pen lightly on the table and glanced at his watch.

Was he worried we wouldn't start on time or worried because Jarrod wasn't here yet?

He shouldn't be concerned. Jarrod wasn't someone who was

rigidly prompt. He was early, late, or exactly on time depending on which he thought would serve him better.

Today that meant he probably wanted to appear on time to make an entrance. He wouldn't be late. That would potentially annoy the judge and bias him or her against Jarrod's side.

Jarrod's lawyer glanced over at me. He nodded his head, leaned across the gap, and extended his hand. "Mrs. Miller."

His hand had a soft look to it, but everything inside me recoiled, as if he were extending a piece of raw meat. He knew what Jarrod had done to me. Even if Jarrod hadn't told him, he'd know what I had put in the petition for divorce. Yet he chose to represent him anyway.

I tucked my hands between my knees. "I'd rather not."

The man's eyebrows raised slightly, but he pulled his hand back. My dad would have said that was rude of me. He'd have been right. But sometimes guilt by association was true. You picked who to tie yourself to in business and in life. What they did reflected on you whether you liked it or not.

And I had the right to choose who touched my body, even if only through a handshake.

Behind me, Claire made a sound like she was trying to muffle a laugh. At least she approved.

The judge entered, and we all rose.

He greeted Mr. Kirkland and me, then settled his gaze on Jarrod's lawyer. "Mr. Butler, where's your client?"

Mr. Butler set his pen aside as if consciously trying not to fidget. "He must be stuck in traffic, Your Honor. He's a conscientious citizen, and he doesn't use his phone while driving."

His excuse felt hollow. All new cars came equipped with Bluetooth capabilities.

He didn't know where Jarrod was, and that was the best he was able to come up with.

I swiveled around in my chair. *Should I be concerned?* I mouthed to Dan.

He shrugged, but wrinkles formed between his eyes.

Not knowing where Jarrod was couldn't be a good thing. He couldn't get to Janie. She was across the country, and we'd checked in with her grandparents before we left for the courthouse. Scott and our other employee were minding the store. Jarrod wasn't likely to do anything to the store in broad daylight with customers around, anyway. And I couldn't think of a reason why he'd want to burn our house down.

What else did that leave? The car?

I turned fully in my seat and motioned to Dan. He came forward and knelt down beside me.

"You need to check the car. Jarrod could be out there now cutting the brake lines or doing something else to make sure we don't make it home alive."

Dan nodded and left the courtroom without another word. A warm swell filled my chest. He was so much the opposite of Jarrod in every way.

"Where's your client, Mr. Butler?" the judge asked. "I'm not going to hold this up all day. I have other cases to hear."

"Ten more minutes, Your Honor. He'll be here. I spoke to him last night and confirmed the time with him. He must be having car trouble."

Yeah, with sabotaging our car if I were right. His lawyer probably had no idea. Lawyers weren't immune if they helped a client commit a crime, so Jarrod wouldn't have risked telling his lawyer and having the man turn him in.

I stared at my watch, another five minutes ticking past.

Maybe I shouldn't have asked Dan to check the car. He didn't have his service weapon with him. He hadn't wanted to risk anymore accusations by Jarrod, so he'd dropped it off at the police station and planned to pick it up again on the way home. We hadn't planned to split up. Now I'd sent him outside alone and unarmed.

I squirmed in my seat and watched another minute pass.

Dan came back in, and I slumped back in my chair. I hadn't sent him out into an ambush after all.

He leaned close to my ear so only I could hear. "I didn't see anything, but I called a friend of mine who works the motor pool for the department. He's on his way. He'll make sure we won't have any unpleasant surprises."

I slumped slightly in my chair. Dan squeezed my hand and then went back to his seat.

"Your client has five more minutes, Mr. Butler," the judge said. "No more."

Behind me, Claire and Dan whispered low enough that I couldn't hear their words. He was probably filling her in on why he'd briefly left.

I stared at my watch again. One minute. Two. Five.

"That's it." The judge shuffled the papers on his desk. "I'm confirming the divorce of Amy Miller and Jarrod Miller according to the conditions outlined in the petition for divorce submitted by Amy Miller. Have a nice day."

The judge left.

Mr. Kirkland collected up his papers. "That went much better than expected."

My body felt too numb to stand. "Is that it? I'm not married anymore?"

He smiled down at me in a way that reminded me of my dad. "There's a bit of paperwork to file, but yes, essentially."

All the bones in my body felt like they'd gone to liquid. We hadn't had to prove that I wasn't mentally incapable. We hadn't had to prove all the things he'd done.

It felt almost anticlimactic, not that I was complaining. The statements from the pastor and his wife and the woman who ran the woman's shelter would still help with my restraining order if I needed one in the future. They could also help prove Jarrod shouldn't be given power of attorney over me if he continued trying to get me deemed incompetent.

As we filed out of the room, Mr. Butler said something into his phone that sounded like "where are you?" but the way he kept talking made me think he'd gotten Jarrod's voicemail.

Dan slid an arm around me and drew me into his side. I instinctively started to hold myself back and then stopped. I wasn't married anymore. Dan and I weren't breaking any vows.

I leaned into him instead. "I can't figure out why Jarrod didn't show up."

Dan looked down at me. His eyes held so many promises that I would have stopped and kissed him right there had it not been an inappropriate place and time. "He couldn't have stopped the divorce. Maybe he decided to save face by not having everyone hear about what he'd done to you. The judge we got today is known for encouraging battered women to press charges against their abusive spouses, even if a few years have passed since the last assault."

Backing down was just so contrary to what I knew of Jarrod, but Dan could be right. Jarrod would protect his reputation at any cost.

Mrs. Kirkland came up on my other side. "How does it feel?"

How was I supposed to feel? Most people probably weren't happy about a divorce, even if they'd wanted it and were relieved it was over. Very few people got married knowing or hoping it would end. I certainly hadn't. I didn't feel happy or sad or even relieved.

I just felt numb. "I don't think it's sunk in yet."

And we still had so far to go. My divorce wasn't a checkmate. We still had to find a way to keep me safe from Jarrod long term. Zee's death was still unsolved, and Jarrod might have been behind that. It seemed premature to have any feelings since they might need to change.

We exited the building. A man I vaguely recognized from the aborted murder mystery weekend had the hood of Dan's car open. He slammed it shut.

"Everything looks good. I even crawled around underneath." He pointed at his damp clothes. "Your car's in better shape than most of the cruisers I see."

"Thanks." Dan gave him one of those man-slaps on the bicep. "I owe you a coffee as soon as I'm back at work."

"Bring me one of your girlfriend's cupcakes, and we'll call it even."

His girlfriend...oh. Heat rushed into my cheeks. He meant me. He meant me, and I could be that now. That part definitely felt good.

Dan wore a grin that was almost goofy in size.

"Any particular flavor?" My voice came out a little wobblier than I intended. "I'll bake you a whole dozen."

"I'm a traditional chocolate guy, but my wife likes those coffee-flavored ones you make with the whipped cream on the top."

He meant the tiramisu. "I'll pack up some of each. If you

don't want to wait until Dan's back at work, swing by the bakery and I'll send a coffee for your wife as well."

Dan's friend grinned at me and headed off.

"Let's get home," Claire said. "I have a celebration dinner to cook. I invited some guests."

That probably meant Eve—she must have planned lunch with me tomorrow so I wouldn't suspect—Blake, Stacey, and a few of the other Cartwright cousins that I'd gotten to know.

Claire had meant it as a nice gesture. I shouldn't feel disappointed that I wouldn't get to spend the evening alone with Dan.

Dan opened my door for me. Instead of closing it when I climbed in, he leaned over and buckled me in.

He brushed a kiss against my cheek. Shivers shot down into my belly.

"Tomorrow will be for us," he whispered. "I have a few surprises of my own planned."

14

I'd been right about Claire filling the house with people. She went straight to the kitchen to prepare, and within an hour, appetizers spread across the table. Shortly before five o'clock people started ringing the doorbell.

By the time all the guests had arrived, the house was stuffed full of the Cartwright cousins I'd become friends with, Eve, Mr. Wendt who'd owned the bakery before us and had become a kind of mentor, and Alan Brooksbank and his wife. Claire must have even invited Elijah Wells because a bouquet of two dozen yellow roses came to the door amid the other guests arriving.

The card matched Elijah's formal way of speaking. *I hear congratulations are in order. I hope this new phase in your life brings you every happiness.*

Haley Cartwright dropped into the seat next to me on the couch and balanced her plate of food on her knees. She'd put a new blue stud in her nose. It made her look a little like she had magical powers.

"So," she popped a mini quiche into her mouth whole, chewed, and swallowed it down. "How do you feel? The way I hear it, your ex was a bigger a—" She cast a glance in her mom's direction. "A bigger jerk than Claire's ex."

Mrs. Kirkland had asked me the same thing at the courthouse, as had a couple of other people since everyone started to arrive. I still didn't know. The most honest answer was I felt like I was walking in a dream and not quite fully taking part.

My heart rate kept spiking oddly too, racing and making it hard for me to breath. I wasn't married to Jarrod anymore, but he was still out there. Not contesting the divorce was no doubt part of some plan he'd come up with to hurt me worse than he could have had he continued to fight the divorce.

So I wasn't married to him anymore. But I also wasn't completely safe or free yet. Hopefully, the attempted mass murder would eventually send Jarrod to prison for life, and I wouldn't ever have to see him again.

Haley was still looking at me waiting for an answer. I glanced down at my plate of food. "Hungry."

Haley laughed so loud that her mother shot her a look that said *did I raise a hyena?*

The doorbell rang, and then someone pounded on the door as well.

My hands went so cold they almost felt numb. The combination felt unnecessarily forceful. Like the person on the other side was too important to wait and see if we heard the bell.

Claire and Dan exchanged a look. Claire gave a tiny shake of her head. She hadn't invited anyone else.

I got up and set my plate on the couch. We'd only had two people who seemed to keep showing up. The first was Claire's Mike. The second was Jarrod.

Dan strode toward the door. I stood next to the couch. I probably looked odd standing there, staring at the door. But my body didn't seem to want to move, either to follow Dan or to sit back down.

Dan would know what to do and say. He wouldn't allow Jarrod in. If he had to, he'd call the police.

And Jarrod wasn't stupid or reckless enough to try something with all these witnesses.

I forced myself to sit next to Haley again and balance my plate on my knees. My throat was too tight to swallow any of it.

The voices in the room were too loud for me to hear any voices coming from the hall. Unless I wanted to go see for myself, I had to wait.

Dan came back into the room. Two unfamiliar police officers followed him. They had to be police officers even though they were wearing suits. They carried themselves like detectives, somehow taking up more space in the room than was their due. A badge also hung visibly on the belt of the taller one.

The plate tilted and slipped from my knees. Haley caught it before all the food could spill off.

She cursed slightly. "What's going on? Are those friends of Dan's?"

Dan's expression looked chiseled from granite. This had to be about the charge Jarrod had brought against him. They wouldn't find a quiet place to talk to him in the house right now, and it was too cold to talk outside.

Dan led them over to me. His lips were tight. His eyes found my gaze and caught, as if he were trying to tell me something or prepare me for something. If there'd been space on the couch, he probably would have moved to sit beside me. As it was, there wasn't.

A small, cool hand slipped into mine instead. I glanced in its direction. Haley.

"Are you Mrs. Miller?" the taller of the two officers asked.

"I am." The words came out soft and garbled. "I am," I said more forcefully.

Bit by bit the conversation in the room stilled until everyone seemed to be watching.

"Mrs. Miller it's my sad duty to inform you that your husband, Jarrod Miller, was murdered."

15

*J*arrod was murdered?

I repeated the words over to myself. They didn't make sense.

"You're sure?" I knew the words were mine, but they sounded far away.

"Yes, ma'am." The shorter detective spoke this time. They had to be detectives based on their suits. "We were able to identify him from his driver's license. We double-checked with his FBI file."

Jarrod was dead.

A laugh bubbled up inside me. I tried to stuff it back down. I shouldn't laugh. His death wasn't funny. It didn't make me happy.

But my body felt lighter than I could remember feeling in the last decade. My whole body had that same feeling as when you'd been clenching your teeth or balling your hands into fists and you don't even realize it until you let go.

The laugh came back, and I couldn't stop it. I must sound crazy, but I couldn't stop.

He wasn't ever going to hurt me or anyone else again. He wasn't ever going to be able to hurt Janie or Dan or Claire or Nicole or anyone else because of me.

My laughter died, and my cheeks felt wet. He also wasn't ever going to have a chance to redeem himself, either. Or apologize. Or confess to what he'd done so that an innocent person wasn't blamed for his crimes.

Someone had removed the plate from my lap, and someone else who smelled like lavender soap had her arms around me.

Claire and Stacey's voices accosted the detectives for breaking the news to me like that without softening the blow at all. Their voices sounded far away too.

I ran out of air, and tears streamed down my face. I gasped for air. I tried to tell someone that I couldn't breathe, but the words were trapped inside.

A hand pressed into my back, leaning me over my knees.

Dan's face was beside mine. He must be kneeling on the ground. "You need to try to breathe, sweetheart."

"Should I get her a bag?" Haley asked. "That's what they always give people on TV."

Dan must have nodded because the next thing I knew he was holding a paper bag up to my mouth. Slowly, the gasping that I couldn't control eased, and I could draw in a full, normal breath again.

I took the bag from Dan, breathed into it a few more times, and straightened up.

The room was emptier than it had been before. Blake and Alan and their wives had left. So had Mr. Wendt. I could pick out four distinct voices from the kitchen. Claire, Stacey, Eve, and Haley's mom Wendy must be cleaning up and putting away the food.

Haley still sat beside me. Dan got up from his kneeling position on the floor.

Haley scooted down the couch, drawing me with her. Dan took the open spot beside me.

The two detectives had already taken seats.

I glanced over at Haley. She scowled at the detectives as if she wanted to shove them out the door and slam it in their faces. The expression was so at odds with her free-spirited self that it finally made sense why teenage Haley had been the one to stay. When you pushed a normally gentle soul to the point where they felt they had no choice but to be a human shield, no one would be able to talk them out of that role.

I lowered the bag. My neck felt hot. I'd never hyperventilated before. Haley had been right. That was the kind of thing I only expected to see happen on TV. No one I knew in real life had to breathe into a paper bag.

"Are you feeling better, Mrs. Miller?"

I needed to change my name as soon as possible. "Call me Isabel."

The detectives exchanged a look that said the claims Jarrod had made about my incompetence might be true. First, I'd laughed when they told me he was dead, then I melted down completely, and then I asked them to call me by a different name.

"I've been going by Isabel for years to stay hidden from Jarrod. It feels more natural to me now than Amy or Mrs. Miller."

The taller detective pulled a notebook from his pocket and flipped through it. Something about the speed of his movements made me think it was for show. He knew exactly what he wanted to ask me without needing to check any notes.

"I did hear that you'd filed for divorce on the grounds of abuse. It looks like your husband..." He glanced at me. "My apologies, ex-husband, also brought some accusations against both you and Detective Holmes. Can you both account for your whereabouts last night?"

Jarrod had died last night. That explained why he hadn't shown up for the divorce hearing and why his lawyer had no idea what had happened. Jarrod must have been planning to show up. Someone prevented it.

"We were both here asleep," Dan said.

"Together?" the shorter detective asked.

Haley leaned forward slightly as if she were as interested in that tidbit as the detectives were.

"I was in the guest bedroom," I said.

"And I was in my own room," Dan added.

The taller detective jotted something down in his notebook. "Of course you were."

His tone clearly said he already didn't believe us since we were two adults of opposite genders, who rumors linked romantically, staying in a house that belonged to only one of us. The assumption would be that we were sleeping together.

His eyebrows lifted slightly. "So neither of you can be sure that the other didn't sneak out sometime during the night."

The statement was designed to trick us. Either we had to admit we'd lied about separate bedrooms—which we hadn't—or we admitted that neither of us had an alibi for the time of the murder.

They considered both of us suspects. Even if we had spent the night together, we wouldn't have an alibi. They'd instead assume we'd killed him together. They might think that anyway.

"That's true." Dan's voice was cold and sharp as a steel knife.

The sound of it made me shiver. Had I not known Dan as well as I did, I might have thought he had done it. Last night, we couldn't be sure what would happen at the divorce hearing. Nicole said Chief McTavish's friend at the FBI was investigating the doctors who were willing to declare me incompetent, but he wouldn't have any evidence against them before the hearing.

And Dan and I had talked about how a divorce wouldn't stop

Jarrod. He'd escalated too far to simply give up once I wasn't his wife anymore.

If I didn't know for sure I hadn't done it, I might have even suspected myself. Jarrod's accusations against Dan only added fuel to the suspicions.

But I knew I hadn't done it, and whatever anyone else might believe, I knew Dan hadn't done it. Had Jarrod not let me go the night he broke in, Dan would have killed him then, if necessary, to save me. What he wouldn't do was hunt Jarrod down and kill him in cold blood.

The taller detective wasn't looking at me anymore. He'd focused entirely on Dan, and his gaze was as hard as Dan's tone was sharp.

"When was the last time you used your service weapon, Detective Holmes?"

"I drew it last week, when my house was invaded, and I shot it yesterday at the practice range."

He left Jarrod's name out of the home invasion. Wisely. Drawing attention to the animosity between Jarrod and the rest of us wouldn't have been a good move at this point.

Dan's face was impassive now. It was like watching the calm surface of a lake at night. I knew more had to be going on underneath, but he wasn't showing it.

"We'll need to take your weapon with us if you'll kindly tell us where to find it."

Dan rose. "It's locked up in my bedroom. I'll take you to it."

Haley and I sat silently on the couch, arms linked. The conversation from the kitchen had died out as if they'd been listening to what was happening in this room. The floor creaked overhead.

Within minutes, the three men came down again. Dan escorted them out of the house.

He came straight back to where I sat. "Call Nicole."

Something slithery that felt a lot like panic unfurled in my stomach. Dan couldn't have done it, but I couldn't think of any other reason for us to call Nicole than that he thought he was going to need a criminal defense attorney. "Why?"

"Detective Copan has a reputation for false positives. He pushes suspects so hard for so long that they confess just to make it stop. I don't want you talking to him for even five minutes without a lawyer present."

He wasn't concerned about himself. He was concerned about me. Maybe I should have been insulted, but he had good reason to be concerned. If Copan pushed me hard enough that I couldn't think straight, who knew what I'd say simply to make it stop.

"Nicole isn't practicing right now, and it would be hard for her to travel here."

She'd do it if I asked her, which was exactly why I didn't want to ask her.

"She'll be able to recommend someone else," Dan said. "Someone we can trust."

She could do that. Her business partner might even be willing to represent us.

"I'll call her."

Wendy appeared in the door. "Time for us to go, Haley."

Haley glanced at me. "Are you going to be okay?"

No, probably not. Even though Jarrod was dead, he was still managing to hurt us. "I'll be fine."

Haley unhooked her arm from mine. "Call me. Even in the middle of the night if you need anything. I'm up late anyway."

I nodded. The others filed out, passing along similar sentiments, until it was only Dan, Claire, and I still in the house.

Claire locked the door, then dropped into one of the arm chairs. "I thought you were sure Jarrod poisoned our sugar."

Her gaze moved slowly from Dan to me and back again.

Blood pounded in my temples. Was she...she was. She was asking us, without explicitly stating it, if either of us had killed Jarrod.

She didn't want to hurt either of us by asking directly, but some part of her wasn't sure. Dan or I or both of us together made the most sense. Eliminating Jarrod got rid of my problems, and it got revenge for Zee's death—the death of Dan's best friend.

Dan sat on the couch beside me, but he didn't reach for my hand or put his arm around me, as if he wasn't sure I'd want the contact. As if he had a small question that he didn't want to admit that I might think he'd done it.

We both knew our relationship would be over if he'd done it.

Even if he'd done it to protect me. I wouldn't take the risk of being with another man who used violence to solve his problems.

But I'd watched Dan over the past months. Even if everyone else ended up believing he'd killed Jarrod, I wouldn't. Not unless I heard it from his own mouth.

I slid my hand into his. He tightened his grip around it and the muscles in his arm relaxed. He had been worried what I thought.

"I was sure he did it," Dan said. "We might have been wrong."

Jarrod was well respected in his career, but he'd made a lot of enemies by the nature of his job. "Maybe not. It could have been someone else who took an opportunity when they saw one. Someone other than me." I added the last part for Claire's benefit.

She snorted. "Obviously. But those detectives didn't look like they were going to take *someone else did it* as convincing evidence it wasn't one of you two."

No, they definitely hadn't. They'd seemed convinced it was one of us, even if they didn't have the proof they needed yet to arrest one or both of us.

"And," Claire shifted forward on her seat, "it seems like too much of a coincidence that a totally unconnected person would choose now to kill him. How would they even know there'd be an opportunity to kill him and frame you?"

Claire's points were logical as always. Believing that some random person with a grudge against Jarrod had followed him here and timed his murder perfectly to implicate us seemed like a big stretch.

"But then why would the person who actually poisoned our sugar have killed Jarrod?" The question had been rolling around in my head as soon as I started to think clearly again. "He was the perfect cover for what they'd done. By killing him, they've made sure we'll start looking for another poisoner, even if the police don't."

We hadn't been kept in the loop about who the police thought poisoned the sugar. For all we knew, the outside detectives were still looking at me as a possible suspect. Detective Labreck either wasn't being kept up to date on the case or he didn't feel it was ethical to tell Dan anything about what was going on. The only thing he'd told Dan was that he'd started looking into the hotel employees as promised, and he'd continue until Internal Affairs arrived and removed him from the case. That might be sooner rather than later now, given Jarrod's death.

I wanted to rest my pounding head in my hands, but I couldn't. This case had just gotten more complicated.

And if we didn't come up with some answers soon, Dan or I or both of us might end up framed for more than one murder.

16

With Jarrod gone, I packed up my belongings and moved back home with Claire. Staying in Dan's house once the reason was gone would have only confirmed the detectives erroneous suspicions that Dan and I were actually living together. I could understand now why the Bible advised Christians to avoid even the appearance of evil. We opened ourselves up to a lot of rumors.

Dan had also postponed whatever surprise he'd originally had planned to celebrate my divorce. He'd said we'd do it when this case was closed.

Postponing was the right call. I wouldn't have been able to enjoy whatever celebration he had planned with all of this hanging over us.

I'd barely been able to concentrate on work. If we hadn't needed to reopen as quickly as possible to minimize the damage to our reputation, I would have rather taken a sick day. Or a sick week.

But we had to reopen or we'd lose the business. Claire had filed a claim to help replace the ingredients we'd lost, but insurance wouldn't cover the time we'd been closed. Our business was too new to tolerate many financial setbacks.

At least Claire had offered to work the counter so that I could stay behind the scenes. She said my expression wouldn't help instill confidence in our customers.

So far, we'd had a third fewer customers come in than we normally did. We might be innocent, but someone had poisoned our sugar nonetheless. Not everyone wanted to take that kind of risk. Even if they believed we hadn't put the poison in the icing, no one wanted to die accidentally because someone was targeting us or our shop.

I pulled the butter out of the fridge to soften for Elijah's next order of cupcakes. Thankfully, he hadn't abandoned us. Two of our regular clients had called to cancel their orders already. They'd had excuses, but we both knew the truth.

Claire stepped into the kitchen and closed the door behind her. "We have a problem."

I sucked back the hysterical laugh that rushed up inside me. I'd done enough of that when I learned Jarrod was dead, and it certainly hadn't helped my innocence.

"Because we need another one." The words came out a bit more sarcastic than I intended.

"This time it's my ex-husband causing it rather than yours."

I glanced out the round window in the door. I couldn't see Mike anywhere. The only person I could see was a woman in a pant suit standing at the counter. "Is he here again? I can send him away while you deal with the customer at the counter."

Claire planted her hands on her hips. "That's not a customer. That's a PR consultant that Mike apparently hired to help us with some positive press after the poisoning fiasco."

Eve was a marketer, and she was already working on some ideas to help. For free. "Tell her we can't afford to hire someone right now."

"I did that." Claire let out a huff of air. "She told me we couldn't afford not to, but that her fee had already been covered by Mike."

That seemed like an awfully generous move. Mike wasn't known for those. Mike wasn't known for doing anything nice for Claire. "Covered by Mike?"

I knew I probably sounded stupid, but I couldn't think of anything else to say. Maybe I hadn't heard Claire correctly.

"That was my reaction too." She glanced back over her shoulder at the woman still waiting at the counter. "Then I realized this isn't a generous act. He doesn't really care about me or our business. All he wants is a way to stop paying alimony. Since I'm refusing to date the men he's throwing at me, the next best option is for him to make sure our business succeeds. Once I pass the income threshold, he's off the hook for payments. This is a desperate move, even for him."

Had Claire not been so invested in this business for personal reasons, she might have kept it from succeeding just to spite Mike.

He certainly was doing everything he could to wriggle out of continuing to pay alimony. Then again, what he paid for this PR woman was probably a lot less than he had to pay Claire every month. He'd come out ahead in the long run.

He certainly did seem willing to do anything to make that happen.

My breath lodged in my throat. Claire had been the one to make the poisoned icing. We'd assumed Jarrod had laced our sugar with cyanide to hurt me, but what if Mike had done it to get rid of Claire?

"What's wrong with you?" Claire asked. "You haven't responded to anything I said."

"Just..." I couldn't tell her my suspicion. Not until I talked to Dan about it. I was probably being unnecessarily paranoid. No reason to scare Claire unnecessarily. "Just tired."

"I'm going to tell her to leave. We have Eve's help. That's enough."

If she turned the PR woman away, Mike might resort to something more drastic again, the way he had when Claire refused to date the men he sent her way. "I think we should take all the help we can get."

Claire's eyebrows shot up so high they almost disappeared in her hairline.

My throat felt so dry I was sure I wasn't sounding normal. I swallowed. I had to convince her. "You're the one who told me that he owes you. If he wants to hand out money for a PR person for our business, we might as well let him. You supported him while he advanced his career for years. This is him finally paying it back."

Claire frowned slightly. "You're right. It's his money, not ours anyway."

She spun on her heel and marched back into the main part of the shop. I wiped off my hands. I went through the bakery front and into my office. Claire didn't even glance my way. She was already sitting at one of the tables with the PR woman, animatedly telling her why we needed a PR makeover and all the things we weren't willing to do. From the sounds of it, one of the PR woman's first ideas might have been having one of us dress up like a cupcake and stand outside holding a sign. Mike might have hired a PR person, but it seemed like he hired the cheapest one he could find.

I closed my office door and locked it. The locked door would be difficult to explain to Claire if she tried to come in, but that was better than having her overhear my conversation with Dan.

I dialed Dan's number and waited. Each ring felt like it took five minutes rather than a few seconds.

He answered.

"I'm probably being paranoid," I said in lieu of a hello.

"Given how things have been going the last few weeks, you're probably not." His voice had a hint of a smile in it, though not at his usual level.

None of us had smiled much since the day of my divorce hearing. We'd talked about it and decided that Janie should stay with her grandparents until we were sure what was going on. If the police did decide to arrest one or both of us, Janie didn't need to witness it.

"I know that no one likes Mike, but do you think he'd be capable of murder. He's been intent on not having to pay Claire alimony. Do you think...?"

I let the question hang. Dan's end of the call went quiet. My phone didn't beep at me, indicating a dropped call. Otherwise, I would have thought he wasn't there anymore.

"Start from the beginning," he said. "How did you get here?"

One of the things I loved about Dan was how he listened to my ideas. I might be wrong. I might be right. But he took me seriously, even if he eventually wouldn't agree with me.

I went over all the things Mike had done to ensure Claire wouldn't collect alimony. "If he'd having money problems, maybe he got desperate."

Dan drew in a long breath. "I'm not sure. I've known Mike for a long time."

"Known him and didn't like him. Maybe those were your instincts telling you what he was capable of."

A lot of people ignored red flags when they shouldn't. I certainly had. Fear tried to kick in and then stillness settled over me. Jarrod was gone. I wasn't happy he was dead. I wouldn't be happy anyone was dead. And my body would probably still react for a long time, but it was like I'd been in chronic pain, and for the first time in a long time, I didn't hurt anymore.

Dan made the *hmm* noise he defaulted to when he wanted to think. "That wouldn't explain who killed Jarrod. Are you thinking the two are unconnected? Because Mike didn't have a reason to kill your ex-husband."

Was he my ex-husband or was I technically a widow instead? According to the police, Jarrod had died prior to our divorce hearing. Yet another reason for them to think I'd had something to do with it. If Jarrod didn't have a will, or hadn't bothered to change the last will I knew about, I'd inherit everything.

The thought made me queasy. I'd meant it when I told Claire I didn't want anything from Jarrod. I certainly didn't want to look at something in the future and know I'd bought it with his money.

But that was a problem for another day. We had enough to deal with right now without borrowing trouble, as my dad would say.

Mike had a reason to kill Claire, but no real reason to kill Jarrod. The only one I could come up with felt flimsy, even to me. "Claire did tell him that she didn't have time to date because she was helping me through a divorce. He could have thought killing Jarrod would clear her schedule."

"That's a stretch."

"I know." I rolled my chair back and forth, the motion soothing. "Claire just seems so sure that Mike won't stop until he finds a way to get out of paying her alimony."

"I'm sure she's right, but that means he definitely wouldn't have put cyanide in the sugar. He couldn't guarantee it would kill Claire. He knows better than anyone that she rarely eats sweets. Poisoning the sugar was more likely to hurt your business than to hurt her physically."

And other than Claire dying, he could only get out of paying her alimony if she remarried or if her annual income exceeded a certain amount. Hence the PR rep he'd sent to help us with the business. He wouldn't have wanted anything to harm our business.

I sucked in a breath. "What if Mike thought someone else was going to destroy our business?"

"Then I don't know what he might have done." Dan's voice had lost any levity it'd had at the start of the conversation, when he seemed to think my idea was far-fetched. "If he saw someone jeopardizing the business or trying to kill you, which would have also destroyed the business, there's a chance he might have done something about it."

17

*M*y phone beeped with a text message as I exited Elijah's building. Delivering his order of cupcakes had taken longer than usual. He'd asked how I was doing, and I'd had to tell him that someone killed Jarrod.

I should have been back at the bakery an hour ago. The text was probably from Claire asking where I was.

I buckled into the car and pulled out my phone.

The text wasn't from Claire. It was from Nicole.

Anderson is on his way. It'll be okay.

I stared at the screen, then scrolled up to my previous messages with Nicole. We'd been able to talk on the phone regularly since Jarrod had died, so there were fewer messages than there might otherwise have been. The last ones had been her texting me encouraging Bible verses the day of my divorce hearing.

I'd called her about Jarrod's death and to ask her if there was anyone she'd recommend in the area in case Dan or I needed a lawyer. She hadn't known anyone off the top of her head. She'd said she'd talk it over with Anderson, her business partner. He'd been practicing in Michigan longer than she had.

Had she misunderstood and thought we needed someone now? That didn't seem likely. Our conversation had been days ago.

She'd probably sent a text to me that was meant for someone else.

To Lakeshore? I typed back.

That seemed like the easiest way to help her figure out her mistake with the least amount of embarrassment.

The three dots indicating she was writing back appeared on the screen, then stopped, then started again.

Yes. I asked him to do it himself. He didn't speak highly enough about any of the defense attorneys there.

Anderson could have done a consult with us over the phone. He'd only be coming here if one of us had been brought in for questioning.

No police had come for me, unless they were waiting back at the store, and Claire had called Nicole for help. But Claire didn't have Nicole's phone number. Only Dan did.

I dialed his number. It went to voicemail.

I dialed Claire instead. If I had to, I'd call Nicole and ask, but she might not know anything more than what she'd already said. Besides, she thought I already knew.

"This woman's an idiot." Claire practically hissed the words, her voice low. "Her idea for a positive PR campaign is to run ads saying we're so good that someone had to resort to murder to remove us as competition."

It wasn't a bad theory if we'd moved onto a street where there was already a bakery, but we hadn't. It was definitely a bad marketing idea. We didn't need to draw more attention to the fact that our food had been poisoned.

The inept PR woman Mike had hired was also not our biggest problem at the moment if I was right.

"Have you talked to Dan today?" I tried to keep my voice neutral.

"I called him earlier to ask if he was eating supper with us tonight, but I haven't heard back from him yet. Why?" A note of suspicion entered her voice.

So Dan hadn't been answering his phone earlier either. If they'd taken him in for questioning, a call to Nicole might have been the only one they'd allowed him to make. Or it might have been the only one he felt comfortable making, knowing whatever calls he made would be listened to and analyzed.

"Why?" Claire's voice jumped up in pitch. "Is something wrong?"

Her mind had probably gone to death. Mine would have in a similar situation. "I got a strange text from my lawyer friend

Nicole about her business partner being on the way here. I think Dan might have been taken in for questioning."

Claire inhaled sharply. "Should we go to the station?"

They wouldn't let us see him. And it could look suspicious. "Let me see if I can figure out what's going on first." Claire would barely be able to think straight while she waited. I know I wouldn't have been able to. "And fire that woman Mike sent. You're right. She's terrible. Eve will come up with something better for us."

Claire exhaled like she was grateful for something she could do to get rid of some of her pent-up emotions.

I disconnected and placed a call to Nicole. She didn't answer.

She'd call back when she saw my number on her phone, but I didn't want to wait.

I tried Dan again. No answer.

I didn't have a lot of other options. Zee would have helped, but he was dead. Detective Austen had seemed sympathetic, but she was still on leave, same as Dan. I needed an inside man or woman to tell me what was going on.

The only person I could think of was Detective Labreck.

Calling the station and asking for him didn't seem like a good idea. The receptionist might not put me through or one of the Internal Affairs people might get suspicious.

He'd called me months ago when he'd been investigating the death of Harold Cartwright, Claire and Dan's grandfather. Detective Labreck had thought I did it and wanted to talk to me. I might have saved his name and number in my contacts so I'd know not to answer his calls anymore.

I scrolled through. I'd put it under D for *detective.*

I hit the call button.

"This is Labreck," he answered.

"It's Isabel Addington...err, Amy Miller."

"You can go by either name with me. I know you're not trying to hide your identity."

My heartbeat slowed slightly. Labreck wouldn't be trying to trip me up in this conversation. That was a nice change.

"Has Dan been brought in for questioning?"

Silence filled his end of the line, which was as good as a *yes,* but I had to know for sure.

"Claire and I haven't been able to get a hold of him, and we're getting worried, given everything else that's happened."

Labreck sighed. "He's here." He didn't necessarily lower his voice, but his voice sounded quieter somehow nonetheless. "I guess you'll find out as soon as you talk to him, so there's no need for me to withhold that information. He's asked for his lawyer, and they're waiting on him to arrive. Dan was smart about it. They're looking to make an arrest today."

Dan must have called Nicole as soon as he was asked down to the station. Thankfully he'd followed his own advice about not speaking to anyone without a lawyer. Labreck seemed to think that the officers investigating were looking to arrest Dan for it.

Detective Copan didn't seem to care about innocence as long as he could get a confession.

"Do they have any real evidence against him?"

Silence again.

"Please." I had no leverage if he chose to stay tight-lipped.

"Motive. They have a motive. You already know it."

To keep me safe. When I filed for divorce, I'd made Jarrod's abuse public record. The police also knew Dan found him in his house. Whether I invited him in or not didn't really matter. If I invited him in, the motive could be jealousy or to protect me from myself if I were considering going back into an abusive relationship. If I hadn't invited him in, the motive was equally as strong. And Jarrod had filed a complaint against Dan, making it look like Dan was teetering on the edge already.

That wasn't what I'd asked, though. "Motive isn't evidence."

"They matched the bullet that killed the victim to a specific weapon." Labreck spoke slowly, as if carefully choosing his words in a way that wasn't technically violating the rules. "That's all I can say. But getting him a lawyer was a good move. No one who's worked with him believes he did it. Unfortunately, we're not the ones investigating."

He disconnected the call before I could push him for anything more.

They had a ballistic match for the bullet recovered from Jarrod's body. When the detectives came to Dan's house, they'd taken his gun. The obvious conclusion was Jarrod had been shot with Dan's gun, but that seemed impossible. Someone must have stolen his gun and then returned it. But how? We'd been careful about arming the house specifically because we were worried about Jarrod finding a way back in.

I dialed Claire again, connected the call through Bluetooth, and put the car into drive.

Claire picked up.

"You should go into the office. Someone else can watch the counter."

Thankfully, because I'd planned to run deliveries today, Abby was working as well.

A door closed on Claire's end. "What's happening?"

I filled her in.

"He was killed with Dan's gun." Claire's voice sounded like I'd told her he had cancer. "They're going to arrest him."

As much as I wanted to deny it, I couldn't. With motive, that kind of evidence, and no solid alibi since Dan could have sneaked out while I was sleeping or asked me to lie for him, the police weren't going to allow him to leave.

"You need to make sure you have people lined up for the rest of this week." It seemed like an overly practical thing to say, but practical was all I could handle for the moment. "I'll be brought in too if they arrest him. They'll want to get me to admit I knew about it."

Claire's breathing hitched. "You didn't...he didn't..."

"No." The word burst out of me without conscious thought. "You don't really think—"

"Of course not, but you said..." Claire actually growled. "Neither of you killed him. You and I both know that."

The bravado that I expected from Claire was back in her voice, but there'd been a second when she wasn't sure. That doubt was probably normal. Even if you knew and loved someone. Wasn't it?

But if Claire had that moment, should I? I'd known Dan for less than a year. She'd known him his whole life.

She'd seen the way he felt about me long before I did. She knew he wanted to protect me.

Maybe I should have wondered if Dan had actually done it, especially given the evidence.

But I didn't.

I didn't because he knew me. He knew that if he killed anyone, it wouldn't matter if I was safe physically. I wouldn't recover emotionally if a man I trusted hunted down another human being and committed premeditated murder. What that broke in me would never be fixed. Trust had been hard fought before this. It'd die a quick death if Dan broke it.

"He didn't do this." I made my words firm enough that not even Claire could argue with them, even if she'd wanted to. "I don't care what evidence they have against him."

"Of course he didn't do this." Claire's tone changed. She

sounded insulted, as if she hadn't had a moment of doubt either. "What do we do about it?"

I'd keep investigating who really killed Jarrod. Anderson might be an amazing lawyer, but he couldn't stay here. Besides, most lawyers weren't like Nicole. Most didn't try to find the real killer alongside getting their client off.

I couldn't tell Claire that. She wouldn't want me to put myself in potential danger, not even to save Dan from going to prison. Either that, or she'd want to help. Claire and investigations were like trying to put peanut butter with oranges.

"Dan might not get bail. He sent Janie away, and that could look like he'd planned in advance to run after killing Jarrod. I have a history of moves, which could make it look like I'd have been willing to run with him. But if they do give him bail, we need to be ready to pay it."

"I can put my house up as a guarantee. I'll figure out how. A police officer isn't safe in prison long."

A police officer wasn't safe in prison at all. If they denied Dan bail, he'd need to be kept in solitary confinement to keep him alive.

"That's a good idea."

Claire's end of the call went quiet, but she didn't hang up. "Don't do anything stupid, okay? I don't want Dan to go to prison for something he didn't do, but I don't want you to get killed trying to rescue him either."

Apparently Claire knew me better than I thought. "I'll be

careful. I'm hoping some of the officers or detectives who know Dan might be willing to bend the rules a bit to help us."

Detective Labreck had already flirted with the line. That should make it easier to convince him to go a tiny bit further, as long as I didn't ask for too much.

---

18

*T*he next two calls I placed to Labreck went to voicemail. I didn't leave a message. My chances of convincing him to help seemed like they would go down if he didn't have to speak directly to me.

As much as I'd hoped to avoid it, I called the police station as well. The receptionist said Detective Labreck was there, and she redirected my call. It went to voicemail as well.

If I wanted to talk to him, I'd have to go down to the station and hope he'd speak to me.

They were only looking at Dan, which meant they weren't looking at Mike. They didn't even know Mike could be an option. And now that they thought Dan had done it, he couldn't suggest Mike to them. It'd look like he was grasping at straws.

The police station was the last place I wanted to go, especially now. Before, it'd been filled with Dan's friends and co-workers. Now those people were interspersed with outside detectives and officer from Internal Affairs.

Detectives and officers who wouldn't believe me, just like Jarrod had always told me.

Only this time, it wasn't that they wouldn't believe me because I was accusing a fellow officer. It also wasn't that they wouldn't believe me because there was something wrong with me.

They wouldn't believe me because they thought they were right, and I was a possible accomplice to a crime.

I could handle that. This wouldn't be the first time someone had thought I'd committed a crime. Lord willing, it'd be the last.

All I had to do was be brave enough to go there and then wait until Labreck agreed to talk to me.

For Dan's sake, I could do this. Jarrod had been wrong about me, but he'd also been right in another way. Police officers did normally want to protect other officers. Everything I'd seen from Labreck said he wanted to help Dan.

I parked the car and walked through the front door with as much confidence as I could project. Hopefully, the acting skills I'd developed thanks to Jarrod would serve me well. I didn't feel confident.

I approached the desk clerk without hesitation. "I need to speak to Detective Labreck please."

She smiled pleasantly at me. If she recognized my voice from the phone earlier, she didn't give any sign of it. Thankfully, no one else was within ear shot.

She picked up the phone. "I'll see if he's available. What's this about?"

I'd prepared an answer for that on the way here. "I'd rather discuss it only with him."

She nodded, again with a manner that suggested my request wasn't abnormal. Maybe it wasn't. She probably saw a lot of weirder events than a woman who wanted to speak with a specific detective about a private matter.

She spoke quietly into the phone, then hung up. "He'll come get you if you want to take a seat."

I didn't want to sit, but I did it anyway. Waiting here felt surreal. I'd had to come in only a few months ago to identify a potential suspect in a different murder. That day, Dan and Detective Austen had been with me.

"Oh, it's you." Detective Labreck's voice pulled me back to the present. "I should have known."

I jumped to my feet. "How's Dan?"

"His lawyer's about thirty minutes out last count, so it won't be long now. I took him a coffee a few minutes ago. He's doing okay all things considered." He glanced over his shoulder as if he expected someone to be eavesdropping on us. "Is that why you came?"

I shook my head.

He sighed. "Follow me."

We passed the desk clerk and headed back into a room filled with desks. Less than half of them were full. I hadn't been behind the scenes at a police station enough to know if that was normal or due to a combination of the holiday season and the regular officers being denied the opportunity to investigate either of the recent murders.

Labreck tapped the back of a chair as he passed. I dropped into it.

He took a seat on the other side of the desk from me. "Dan always spoke about you as a survivor. Someone who'd gone through a lot and came out stronger for it, rather than getting bitter the way so many people do. I think he should have said you were a fighter who didn't know how to quit."

That sounded like a compliment. And yet, not. "I know how to quit and how to give up. I tried that for a lot of years. It didn't do me any good."

Labreck nodded his head in an acknowledging way. "So why do I have a long line of missed calls from you and a visit now?"

I explained the theory Dan and I had started working on regarding Mike just before Dan's arrest. "Or maybe it's not him, but it wasn't Dan either. If you want to find out who actually killed Jarrod, you need to find out who he talked to since he came here and trace his tracks."

The muscles around Labreck's eyes and mouth tightened. "You know I went to the police academy to learn how to do my job, and then I had to pass a detective's exam. So did a lot of the people here. What makes you think you're the first one to think of that?"

His tone wasn't exactly angry, but it was close. My leg bounced. Jarrod would have said I should stick to baking cupcakes.

He wouldn't be wrong. Detective Labreck wasn't wrong either. I didn't have the education that anyone here had. I did have a clearer perspective, despite my biases. "I'm not trying to tell you how to do your job."

He raised his eyebrows in tandem.

I lifted my hands in a sign of surrender. I didn't always know how to say things in a way that wouldn't offend people. "They're ready to make an arrest on Dan really fast. It might have been too fast for them to check all the ingoing and outgoing numbers. I'm wondering if they skipped that step because they were only looking to see if Dan had called Jarrod or received a call from him."

Detective Labreck tapped a finger on his desk. "Go on."

"All I'm asking is if you'd be willing to check the other numbers. I know they didn't find Dan's because Dan never talked to Jarrod on the phone. That doesn't mean one of the other numbers might not be important."

A shadow fell over the desk. "We're not a private investigation service. You can't come in and hire an officer to run down your own vendetta, Mrs. Miller."

I looked up. So few people called me Mrs. Miller that I had no doubt who was standing there.

Detective Copan stared down at me. "Detective Labreck has tried being patient with you, but you need to leave before we have to charge you with impeding an ongoing investigation."

His timing couldn't have been worse. Detective Labreck's expression gave nothing away. I couldn't tell if he was for me or still against me, willing to look into Jarrod's calls or not.

Detective Copan gave a *you're dismissed* chin jerk.

I slowly got to my feet. Detective Labreck wouldn't even make eye contact with me. Not that I could entirely blame him. Helping me could mean putting his job on the line, especially if someone decided to accuse him of tampering with evidence to help Dan.

I turned around, and my gaze locked with Detective Austen. She still wore street clothes. This time she held a small cardboard box in her arms as if she'd come to collect either her belongings or Zee's.

The other two detectives paid her absolutely no attention. She obviously had enough of a legitimate reason to be there that she wasn't constantly watched.

I passed by her and intentionally didn't look in her direction. Maybe I'd chosen the wrong ally. If Detective Austen still had some access to the station, she might be able to poke around in the evidence for Jarrod's case. The question was whether she'd be willing to take that risk or not.

Given how hard she'd been hit by Zee's death, and given that Dan was Zee's best friend, I was willing to wager that she would.

19

*I*f I didn't look into Mike, no one was going to. Now that Detective Labreck had Copan looming over him, he wouldn't take the risk of investigating a case he wasn't assigned to.

My only chance of proving Dan hadn't killed Jarrod was to talk to Mike and get some information that would convince the detectives on the case that he was a better suspect.

But talking to Mike alone definitely wasn't something I was about to do. If he'd killed Jarrod and I came around asking questions, he might think it was worth it to kill me too, despite the harm to Claire's business. Having to pay his wife alimony for the foreseeable future was better than spending the rest of his life in prison for murder.

Mike was selfish to the core and arrogant. I could go to him and say I wanted him to convince me that he'd done enough for

Claire to warrant not having to pay alimony. All I needed was for him to slip up. People often did. It was why most people—innocent or guilty—should ask for a lawyer as soon as they were brought in for questioning by the police. At least, that seemed to be my lesson from everything I'd heard and seen.

Claire wasn't an option to bring with me. If Mike had killed once, already killing Claire might start to seem like the best option.

I just couldn't go alone. I had to convince Detective Austen to go with me.

I exited the police station. Based on the cars I remembered seeing Detective Austen climb into before, she hadn't parked out front this time, probably because all the spaces were full.

I took the alley and strolled through the officers' parking lot behind the building, trying to look like I belonged.

Only one car looked similar enough to be hers.

I stationed myself beside it.

The December cold seeped through my coat. I shivered.

If Dan didn't get bail, we wouldn't be able to bring Janie home for Christmas. How would we ever explain this to her? I couldn't let that happen.

A figure exited the back door of the building and headed toward the car I stood beside.

Detective Austen stopped ten feet away. "What are you doing here?"

Her voice was brittle, like someone who was so close to

snapping that the tiniest tap would break them. Brittle and suspicious. She seemed like a decent cop. She's probably already guessed the answer to her own question.

"Waiting for you," I said. I was shaking so hard—only partly from the cold—that my teeth chattered when I said it. If she wouldn't help me, I was out of options.

She tucked the box under one arm and gestured back at the station. "I meant here."

Time to see where her loyalties lay. "We both know Dan couldn't have killed my ex-husband, but no one will listen to me. So I came to you."

She unlocked her car. I moved aside, and she slid the box gingerly into the back seat. "I expected you would eventually. You have a history of investigating cases that cross your path."

She didn't sound like she respected what I'd done. Not even grudgingly.

That made the situation more difficult. If she thought neither of us should be involved in figuring out who killed Jarrod, and whether Jarrod killed Zee, then she was less likely to help. I'd be out of options. Or, at least, out of options that weren't crazy reckless.

I couldn't give her a chance to turn me down too. I had to show her that I needed her help. That Dan needed her help.

She clearly didn't think I should be investigating, and she must have some pride in her own abilities as a detective. If I appealed to that, I might have a chance. I'd show her that all was lost without her. "Too many pieces don't add up. Dan doesn't leave his gun lying around where anyone could get it, so how was it used in the murder, for example? You were in love with his best friend. You can't leave him to spend the rest of his life in prison, assuming he lives that long."

She stared at me, and I stared back. I couldn't back down. She was my last hope.

She closed the back door of her car so softly that it didn't even make a thump. "Get in the car. We can't talk about this here."

My car—technically Claire's car—was parked out front, leaving her without a vehicle if she needed one. She'd be at the bakery for a few more hours at least, though. Detective Austen and I shouldn't be that long, and presumably she'd drop me back here after we were done. Besides, if I tried to drive separately, she might change her mind.

I climbed into the passenger seat.

Detective Austen surveyed the parking lot, as if she didn't even want to be seen together for fear of what would happen to her job. She finally slid in as well and started the car.

She pulled out of the lot. "How did you figure it out?"

It? That wasn't very specific.

"Or maybe a better question is how much do you know?" Detective Austen asked.

The detectives investigating the case must know more than I did about the details. Hopefully once I filled Detective Austen in on what Dan and I had pieced together before he was arrested, she'd have information that could help sort this out and point to Mike.

"We watched the security tapes for my bakery, and there wasn't any opportunity for someone to poison the sugar there. So we—Dan and I—realized it had to be done at the hotel right before the murder mystery weekend. We took Jarrod's picture and showed it to the staff. No one recognized him. That's when we knew it had to be an inside job."

Detective Labreck had said he'd check into the backgrounds of the employees. Who knew if he'd done that or how far he'd gotten if he had. "Jarrod wasn't above blackmail, bribery, or intimidation."

Detective Austen's hands tightened and released on the steering wheel. "Blackmail. He had ways of searching records as an FBI agent that no one else would have access to."

True enough. Blackmail did make the most sense. Bribery or intimidation could create a situation where someone could have turned the tables on him and become a blackmailer themselves. But if Jarrod was the one doing the blackmailing, he'd have the employee in a corner. People would do awful things to keep their secrets hidden.

"He said it was a laxative." Detective Austen's voice was flat enough that Amazon's Alexa or Apple's Siri sounded more life-like. "It was supposed to ruin your business, not kill anyone."

I straightened. Detective Austen had been conducting her

own investigation, despite being on leave. I should have guessed it. Maybe Labreck had told her which employees might be a possibility for blackmail, and she'd already spoken to them.

I opened my mouth to ask why she hadn't coordinated with Dan. She should have known she could trust him.

I shifted slightly in my seat, so I could see her better. Her fingers were too tight on the wheel. Her knuckles stood out white.

She turned onto one of the main roads that led out of town.

Fear raised his head. *Something's not right here.*

I'd already figured that much out. I didn't need him to confirm it.

We passed the city limits. Detective Austen picked up speed. Not enough to get pulled over if we passed a police officer running radar, but fast enough to put extra distance between us and town.

Dear God, no. She couldn't have.

And yet, her being the one who mixed cyanide into the sugar made more sense than her convincing one of the hotel employees to talk to her. Even more than her taking the risk of talking to one of the employees when that might result in a mistrial down the road. She wouldn't have risked an accomplice in Zee's murder walking free.

Unless she was the accomplice.

She must think I'd already figured it out.

I ran everything I'd said back through my head. I hadn't

mentioned Mike yet. Everything I'd said could have been misconstrued by someone with an already guilty conscience, in the same way that I'd almost been deceived because I came into this thinking Detective Austen was my ally.

I looped my arms around my waist and tucked my hands under my elbows as if I were cold. My phone was a hard bulge in my pocket. I suddenly understood what a dehydrated man surrounded by salt water felt like. My phone was so close and seemed like salvation, but it was also completely out of reach. She wasn't going to let me pull it out and call or text someone.

I had to be sure before I did or said anything rash. Before we got any further away from Lakeshore, and safety, and help.

I also needed evidence. Otherwise, assuming I survived, it would be her word against mine. Jarrod had told me how that would go.

I edged my phone out of my pocket and wiggled it down onto the seat beside me, close to the door. I pretended like I was shifting on the seat and tapped the voice recorder app. Detective Austen was farther away than I'd ever tried to record myself, but it was my only shot.

"He said it was a laxative," I repeated.

Her head bobbed once, sharply. "I wouldn't have done it otherwise. I would never have risked my friends. All those people I worked with and their families. Zee." Her voice had taken on a you-have-to-believe-me tone. "Somehow he'd found out about...in my first year on the job, I accidentally shot someone. He had his hands up, and then he sneezed and moved reflexively to cover his mouth. It was the first time I'd ever had to draw my weapon, and I was so nervous. I pulled the trigger without thinking. He'd moved so suddenly. My partner and my captain helped me cover it up. My career would have been over had anyone found out."

A single mistake. She'd said something about that to Dan when she called him about drawing his weapon on Jarrod.

Jarrod must have dug into the background of every officer on the Lakeshore police force until he found one with something he could use against them. Detective Austen's job would have been over then had anyone found out what truly happened, and it would be over now.

Putting some laxative into the sugar must not have seemed like a big deal in balance with that. She'd been there setting up anyway. No one would have thought anything of her moving around anymore than they would have suspected a hotel employee. We'd been right that it was an inside job. We'd just gotten which *inside* wrong.

Laxative wouldn't have hurt anyone long-term. The only thing it would have hurt was our business. We'd have been blamed for giving everyone food poisoning.

"I've worked every day since that shooting to make up for it," Detective Austen said. "I hadn't told anyone. Not even Zee."

Her voice wobbled on his name.

Unintentionally, she'd killed the man she loved. Jarrod had

lied to her. I believed her when she said she wouldn't have gone through with it if she'd known what she was actually putting in the sugar. She wouldn't have done it even if it cost her career.

Until she killed Jarrod, both of the murders she'd committed had been accidents and unpremeditated.

Jarrod's murder was different. She'd crossed that line. It'd seem like a logical step to continue covering it up by killing me too.

Whatever reason she had for bringing me out here couldn't be a good one. I had to make her believe I sympathized with her. "Jarrod was always a liar and a manipulator. A lot people probably wanted him dead but weren't brave enough to do anything about it."

She eased her foot off the gas slightly. Her gaze slid sideways. "What do you want? You know I can't confess. It won't be any better for me in prison than it will for Dan, and a good lawyer might still get him off. So what are you hoping to get out of this?"

Coming in, I'd been hoping for an ally to confront Mike, who I thought was the person who actually killed Jarrod.

Now? Well, now I had no idea what I wanted except to be out of this car and away from Detective Austen.

She, however, clearly thought I'd come here to blackmail her. If I had, I was the stupidest blackmailer ever to get in a car with her. "Did you leave any holes that we could use to cast reasonable doubt when Dan goes to trial?"

"Sorry." Her voice sounded anything but. "I'm not going to tell you that. Anything I give you will be more evidence you have to use against me. How much will it cost for you to keep quiet?"

No amount of money in the world. Not even if she offered me a million dollars. Not even if she guaranteed no one would ever find out. Because I'd still know and God would still know. The morality of the world might change every decade, but God never changed, and taking money to cover up a crime would definitely disappoint him.

Detective Austen didn't know me, though. She clearly thought I could be bought. I had to let her think that for now.

"I don't want enough that it'd be noticed. That wouldn't be good for either of us."

I had no idea what was too high or too low for a blackmailer offering to cover up evidence of a murder. Maybe if I didn't give an amount she'd make an offer.

She was still driving us further out of town, though.

My hands felt numb, and tingling crept up my arms as if I'd pinched a nerve. She was stalling too by offering me money. Wherever she was taking me, she wanted me to go quietly, without trying to get away. She had no intention of taking me back to town alive.

Actually, she had no intention of taking me back to town at all. My body was going to end up far away, where no one could tie her to the crime.

No one had seen me leave with her. I'd made sure of that by sneaking out to her car and waiting for her rather than speaking to her inside the police station.

We had no prior friendship that would make anyone suspect her in my death. An exceptionally savvy investigator might ask her if she blamed me for Zee's death, looking for a motive there. She'd have an easy response, though. Hadn't the police already crossed Claire and me off the list? At the very least, we weren't primary suspects.

She still hadn't responded to my last sentence.

"What do you think would be a fair amount?" I asked.

I held back a flinch. Technically, nothing was a fair amount for a blackmail. Fair didn't even come into it.

She glanced at me at the same time as I glanced at her. Her gaze didn't shift away as rapidly as it had before.

She knew that I knew.

She sighed. "I'm going to make it as quick and painless as I can, okay? I never wanted to do this. Your husband forced me into all of this. I'm a good person."

How many murderers told themselves that? Sure, I killed so-and-so, but I take care of my mother so I'm a good person, or I'd never hurt a kid so I'm a good person, or I had no other choice so I'm a good person.

The Bible was right. At our core, none of us were good people. We were all selfish and in need of the sacrifice Jesus made to save us from ourselves.

I certainly wasn't a good person. Not on my own. Even when I tried my best, I fell short. I'd never understood when people argued that all good people went to heaven when they died. How could you even tell what made someone good enough? Dan and I would probably both be considered "good people," but we lied and hurt others—intentionally and unintentionally. All those people who came up with a list of excuses for killing someone else thought they were good people, too.

At least if I died today, though, I could do it knowing where I'd spend eternity. Detective Austen didn't have that assurance. And one day, when all of this caught up to her, she might very well take her own life. "You can still make this right. You don't have to make things worse by killing me. Killing me is only going to make you feel worse. The guilt will eat you alive."

"You think confessing and spending the rest of my life in solitary confinement in prison is going to make me feel better?" Her tone said *you really are crazy.*

"It'll be a first step, but the real peace—"

"You're really going to spend your last minutes trying to convert me to your religion? You and Dan are a good couple."

I opened my mouth to tell her that it wasn't a religion. It was a relationship with a person.

Her look made me stop. Not only wasn't she listening, but every word I said seemed to solidify her decision to kill me.

I wasn't going to change her mind—about faith or anything else.

That left me with no option but to figure a way out of this. I had to stop her. Not only to save myself, but also because she'd crossed a dangerous line. With the way she looked at everything she'd done, it'd be easy to cross that line again and again if it served her. The next person who came around asking questions she wasn't comfortable with would find the same fate as I was about to.

Not to mention that Dan would spend his life in prison for a crime he didn't commit, and Janie would lose a second father. Losing a first one was hard enough on anyone.

And Claire. What would happen to Claire if I disappeared and Dan went to prison? Would she ever recover from that? Would she think I'd abandoned them both?

I couldn't give up.

My phone wasn't an option. I had no illusions about what the bulge under her jacket was. If I went for my phone, she'd shoot me and then find a way to dispose of the car later. Not only did she have the advantage of knowing exactly what she'd need to do to effectively destroy evidence, but she had all the time in the world.

She didn't have to be into work, so no one would miss her. Claire would eventually report me missing, but I had a history of disappearing. She'd have a hard time getting the police to take her seriously. By the time anyone did, Detective Austen would have easily destroyed or cleaned up any evidence.

I couldn't jump out of the car. Her car was modern enough

that the doors locked as soon as she put the car into drive. Besides, I wouldn't survive throwing myself out of a car moving at this speed. No sense in doing her job for her. At the very least, I'd be injured enough that I'd be easy to finish off.

But maybe it wasn't important whether or not I survived as long as I stopped Detective Austen. Maybe risking my life was worth it if I incapacitated her at the same time.

Trees and telephone poles lined the road we were on. If I grabbed the wheel, I might be able to crash the car. My chances of surviving that were at least equal with hers. And I'd be close enough to her that she wouldn't be able to pull her gun and shoot me.

If I managed to stay conscious after the crash, I could call for help.

Not the greatest plan, but it was what I had.

First, I had to distract her enough that she wouldn't suspect anything was coming. Wrestling a wheel away from someone probably wasn't as easy as it appeared on TV. My timing had to be just right.

"Are you going to shoot me?" I didn't have to try to add wobble to my voice. It was already there.

She shook her head. "Ballistics would be able to match the bullet to my gun whenever they finally find your body. I don't plan to make that easy, but I also can't risk it'll happen in my lifetime." She sounded so clinical.

What could I ask her that would hold her attention? "How

did you manage to get away with it when you killed Jarrod? The police found a match to Dan's gun."

"I swapped it with mine when we went to the shooting range together."

That made sense. They'd both been given standard issue weapons. They'd look identical if someone didn't examine them for the serial number or any small imperfections. "But when they collected his gun from his house, it wasn't still yours."

"I switched them back while you were at your divorce hearing. I convinced Dan that he should leave his weapon at the station. That way, your soon-to-be ex couldn't accuse him of anything else. If he did, Dan would be able to prove that his weapon hadn't even been on him at the time."

We'd made the stop at the police station before and after the hearing. Dan had explained his reasoning, but he hadn't mentioned the idea came from Detective Austen. He must have thought she was looking out for him.

She'd been so smart and careful about it all.

"I thought Dan was your friend."

She kept her eyes on the road. "Dan was Zee's friend."

It was now or never. I lunged as far as my seatbelt would let me, grabbed the wheel with both hands, and tugged.

20

The car swerved toward the side of the road. Detective Austen cursed. Her elbow shot up and slammed into my eye. She jerked the wheel back in the other direction.

Hot pain burst through my face and skull as if I'd been set on fire. My body wanted to let go of the wheel. But I knew pain. I'd learned how to lock pain away so I could do what I needed to. It was the one useful gift Jarrod had given me.

I put up my mental walls and faked loosening my grip, so she wouldn't be expecting my next move. Then I heaved on the wheel again.

The car hit the edge of the road, and the world spun. My body wrenched against the seatbelt.

A deafening sound of crunching metal and then everything went black.

~

I FORCED MY EYES OPEN, BUT EVERYTHING AROUND ME WAS STILL dark. I was lying on my side. Sort of. The position didn't feel right. Nothing felt right. My whole body ached and burned. I couldn't tell what was wrong or where.

And I was so cold. Shivers sliced over me, sending new waves of pain in their path.

Detective Austen. The car crash. Everything came back to me slowly in bits.

I'd succeeded. I just hadn't realized it would feel like this.

The car wasn't running anymore, which was probably for the best. We didn't need the fuel tank catching fire or a plugged tail pipe filling the cabin with carbon monoxide.

I eased my head to look upward. Detective Austen dangled above me, suspended by her seatbelt.

The car must have flipped or tipped and was now lying on its side. The airbags had deployed. I could make out the white sacks, like deflated balloons, hanging from the dash.

How long had passed since the crash? If she'd had some sort of roadside program that notified authorities if her airbags deployed, shouldn't they be here by now? It'd been daylight when we left Lakeshore.

No one was coming, and everything hurt.

The pain was a good sign in a way. I wasn't paralyzed. I wasn't dead.

I stilled as much as I could. Detective Austen's ragged breathes filled the silence. She wasn't dead either.

We needed help.

My phone had been next to me. I'd wedged it between me and the seat. Maybe it was still there, on the side of me that was pressed against the car door.

I reached my left hand around, trying to move as little as possible. My fingers touched something cold and smooth. It was still there.

I slid my phone out. Something about it didn't look right.

I pressed the Home button. The screen lit up, but the light flickered, and cracks spiderwebbed against the front.

This wasn't good. I didn't know where Detective Austen kept her phone, even if I could unbuckle and search the car with my injuries. Her phone might not have survived the crash either.

A weird little laugh built in my chest, and I tamped it down. I did not survive Jarrod, a handful of other crazy murderers, and a car crash only to die of hypothermia.

I sent up a wordless prayer and pressed the Home button on my phone again. It stayed on long enough to take my passcode. One step down.

I tapped in 9-1-1, but the screen went black before I could hit the dial button. Even if I was able to keep my phone alive long enough to reach a human being, I didn't know exactly where we were. I knew we'd been headed out of Lakeshore and the general direction, but I'd been too distracted by the conversation with Detective Austen to watch for crossroads.

And if my phone died for good halfway through the call, they wouldn't even be able to track it. Without knowing where to search, the 9-1-1 operator might write me off as a lost cause. Too many other people needed help every minute.

I couldn't call 9-1-1. I needed to call someone who wouldn't give up on me.

Dan was still likely in custody, so I couldn't try him.

The fewest steps gave me the best chance of my phone staying on long enough. I pushed the Home button again. My screen blipped to life. I quickly touched the phone icon and then went to recent calls. Hit redial for Detective Labreck.

And prayed that he wasn't somehow involved in all this.

"Isabel?" His voice crackled. He hadn't let it go to voicemail, and he'd skipped the hello, as if he'd been waiting for my call. "Claire...looking...where are..."

More must be wrong with my phone. Who knew how much he'd hear. "We need help. Outside Lakeshore. Detective Austen kidnapped me. She killed Jarrod, and I crashed her car."

No answer. Not even static.

I moved the phone away from my ear. The screen was black again. I'd keep calling Detective Labreck as many times as I could until he understood.

I pressed the Home button again. Nothing happened. My phone was dead.

That'd been my last hope. The police couldn't track a phone if it wasn't turned on.

I'd have to look for Detective Austen's phone.

Unbuckling the seatbelt felt like asking my body to run a marathon. My right arm was pinned under my body, so I swiveled as much as I could and released the belt with my left hand.

The belt let go. I pushed myself up, and pain flared. I collapsed back onto my side. Black dots flooded my vision. Something worse than a few bruises was wrong with my right arm. Broken? A dislocated shoulder? Whatever was wrong with it, I wasn't going to be able to use it. Not to get up. Not to crawl through a wrecked car in the hope of finding a useable cell phone.

My fate was now in the hands of Detective Labreck and God.

21

J must have passed out again or fallen asleep. The next thing I knew lights moved over the car in strobes and the sound of metal shearing away from metal felt like it was everywhere.

The sound stopped momentarily. "If you can hear me, Isabel, stay still. We'll have you both out as soon as we can."

The voice was male. Not Dan's but familiar.

And then the blackness swallowed me again.

"BIOLOGY MEANS NOTHING. SHE'S MY FAMILY." CLAIRE'S TONE was forceful and shrill. "So you're going to let me in there."

I peeled my eyes open even though they felt like someone had tried to glue them shut. A hospital room took shape around me. And I was warm. My body still hurt but less than it had before. My right arm felt trapped in something. I slowly moved my left arm and touched my right. A sling. I couldn't tell if the hard structure in the sling was a cast or only a solid splint.

A man's voice was saying something to whoever must be blocking Claire's path.

Claire. I wanted Claire. She was right. She was my family.

"Claire?" My voice croaked out too soft for anyone to hear. I swallowed and tried again. "Claire!"

The hospital staff member must not have been fast enough to stop her because Claire burst into the room.

"They weren't going to let me see you." Claire dropped into the chair next to my bed as if it'd been placed there specifically for her. "I told them they either let me in or I'd be sleeping in the hallway until you woke up."

I had no doubt Claire would have followed through with her threat. She got what she wanted.

Now that she was next to me, I was sure to have someone who would believe me about what happened. If Detective Austen had lived long enough to be rescued, she might be telling a different story.

"Detective Austen was going to kill me because I figured out she killed Jarrod."

"We figured it had to be something like that." Detective Labreck appeared in the doorway. His suit was rumpled, as if he'd been wearing it too long.

I glanced at Claire. Her hair had a sag to it as well, and a white swipe that looked like flour smeared across one of her thighs. More time must have passed than I realized, but she hadn't bothered to change.

My mind was noisy with questions. "How did you find us?"

Labreck moved to stand beside Claire's chair. He placed a hand on the back. The move was a surprisingly familiar one, but Claire didn't shoot him a glare, letting him know to keep his space.

He nodded at Claire. "Claire had come down to the station because you didn't return to work."

"I kept trying to tell them that you wouldn't have disappeared without telling me where you were going, not with everything that'd been happening."

"She refused to leave until we did something about it." He smiled wryly, but there was a warmth to it that I wouldn't have expected. "When the call came in, we could only catch every few words."

"Help. Outside. Kidnapped. Car." Claire rattled them off as if she'd been repeating them to herself for hours. She probably had.

"Unfortunately, I wasn't able to locate your phone using GPS," Labreck said.

My phone dying was one of the last memories I had before waking up here. "It was damaged in the crash."

And none of that explained how they'd found me in the end.

Lakeshore had many main roads leading into it and even more smaller roads.

"That's when I traced Miranda Austen's phone."

Claire gave him a smile that said *brilliant move*.

Maybe I'd received a blow to the head in the crash, but I still wasn't following. "How did you know to do that?"

"From your request. You'd asked me earlier, before we were interrupted, to look at calls going into or out of your ex-husband's phone. I'd recognized Miranda's number when Claire came barging in. I put the pieces together after your disjointed call. I couldn't come up with a legitimate reason for Miranda to be communicating with your ex, especially since it started happening a couple of weeks before the department's murder mystery weekend." He shrugged. "I gambled, and we won."

I hadn't thought he would actually go through with my request. Thank goodness I'd been wrong. If he hadn't seen Detective Austen's phone number in Jarrod's phone, he might not have put two and two together. We could have very well died in that car before anyone found us.

"Is Detective Austen awake?"

Labreck shook his head. "She took a hard blow to the head. The doctors aren't sure..."

My stomach clenched. I hadn't wanted to kill her, but I had been prepared to kill us both if that was what it took to stop her. Still, mentally preparing myself for it and knowing I might have succeeded were two different things.

I shifted into a more comfortable position. As thankful that I was to have walked away alive, and to have stopped Detective Austen from hurting anyone else in the future, it'd feel like a hollow victory if Dan still went to prison for killing Jarrod. "What about Dan?"

Labreck shifted on his feet. "His bail hearing is scheduled for tomorrow."

"Do you have any techs who can pull sound files off of a destroyed phone? I recorded Detective Austen confessing. The audio might be soft, so don't let them discount it if they can't hear it right away."

Detective Labreck jerked slightly. "You thought to record her while your life was in danger."

Claire snickered and rolled her eyes as if he should have expected it.

I shrugged. Pain lanced out from my shoulder. I wouldn't be doing that again anytime soon. "I figured that if I died, at least there'd be evidence of the truth somewhere. If I got out alive, I wanted to be able to prove what had happened."

"You were the one who crashed the car." Labreck's eyebrows went up. "You recorded her and crashed the car so she couldn't get away with it. I can see why Dan likes you. You really are a survivor."

22

It was a good thing I was awake and able to give my permission for visitors because my hospital room should have had a revolving door. Haley and Wendy came. Haley brought her make-up case, and I had to fend off her attempts to cover my bruises. Eve, Blake and his family, Stacey, Elijah, Mr. Wendt, and Alan all came through.

Claire and Detective Labreck had just arrived to fill the space that hadn't been empty for more than a half hour when Nicole called to tell me that Chief McTavish's friend in the FBI had identified the doctors who'd lied for Jarrod.

"As soon as you're back on your feet," she said, "we really want you to come for a visit. It's long overdue."

I promised her I would. I could do that now. I could make promises. I could go places. I could have friends without worrying about Jarrod hurting them to punish me.

I set the phone back in its cradle, and Claire and Detective Labreck both looked at me with expectant expressions. They'd come together again today, and Claire refused to meet my eyes every time I gave her a *what's-going-on-here* look.

I filled them in. "While it didn't matter anymore for me, it still mattered for other people who might be wrongfully deemed incapable in the future if those doctors hadn't been found out."

"And for anyone they made a report on before," Labreck said. "All those people will need to be reassessed."

That was something I hadn't thought of. Perhaps I was the only one. Jarrod had been willing to go to extreme lengths to get what he wanted. He'd also had the means to dig up secrets that otherwise would have remained hidden. The doctors he'd blackmailed might very well have never strayed over the line before. But we couldn't count on it. Not when people's living conditions and freedom were at risk.

Thankfully, that wasn't something I had to handle myself. I could go back to simply being a cupcake baker again. Claire and I were going to have more than enough to handle with our business. I certainly wouldn't be bored.

Claire glanced at the door for the third time since they'd entered my room.

"What's going on?"

She shook her head. "You'll have to learn not to be so suspicious now."

But her voice lacked the reprimand it usually carried when someone did something that annoyed her.

A nurse popped her head into the room. "Time for me to change your dressing."

I'd been in so much pain at the time of the crash that I hadn't even felt the spot where I'd split the skin on my forehead. Thankfully, I'd been able to avoid looking in the mirror in the bathroom. I didn't want to know if I resembled Frankenstein's monster with my stitches and bruises.

The nurse's gaze landed on Claire and Detective Labreck. "More visitors." She chuckled. "I swear your room is busier than someone with ten children. I'll come back in a half hour."

My chest felt warm and full. A year ago I'd been so alone that if I arrived at a hospital without ID, no one would have even been looking for me. I'd have died a Jane Doe.

Even before Jarrod isolated me from the world, I hadn't known what it felt like to have this level of love and support all around me. It'd take years yet before I felt like I deserved it.

Claire glanced back at the door.

I reached out and snagged her wrist. "I know when you're lying, Claire Cartwright."

"She's trying not to spoil the surprise." Dan stepped through the doorway. "I'm officially a free man again, thanks to the recording you made."

I wanted to run to him and throw my arms around him, but

moving still made my body feel like it was going to shatter. The nurses had to help me to the bathroom.

Detective Labreck put a hand on Claire's shoulder. "Why don't we go get that cup of coffee we talked about?"

The way she smiled up at him made her look a decade younger. Mike might end up not having to pay alimony for much longer after all. But if the way Claire and Detective Labreck were looking at each other was any indication, losing her alimony payments would be well worth it.

Dan watched them go and then took the chair next to my bed that Claire had vacated. "When did that happen?"

Smiling hurt, but I couldn't help myself. "While you and I were both busy with other things apparently."

Dan laughed. I'd missed that sound even though it'd only been a few days. There was always something warm and soothing about his laugh. There had been from the first time I met him.

He set a Styrofoam container on my lap. "I brought you something."

I opened the top. The container was filled with onion rings. They smelled delicious, but it seemed like a strange thing to bring. Most people brought flowers or a card or one of those helium balloons to a hospital patient.

Dan slid his fingers through mine. "Do you remember the day at Serial Grillers when we agreed to be partners for investigating Grandpa's death? We shook on it."

I'd never forget that day. I'd been desperate to prove that I hadn't been the one to kill Harold Cartwright, and I'd been convinced that Claire had done it. I'd also been desperately lonely. Even though I wasn't a team player, and I wasn't sure I could trust him, I'd needed an ally.

That handshake had turned out to be the best decision I'd ever made. "I remember."

Dan met my gaze, and his smile was in his eyes as well. "I went back to ask the owner of Serial Grillers another question that day, and you mimed for me to get onion rings."

My face heated, from my cheeks down into my neck. I'd been so hungry back then, and the onion rings had smelled amazing. I knew if he bought some, I could filch a few. My miming was so terrible, though, that it'd taken two tries to get Dan to understand what I meant. "You came back and said you thought I was proposing when we hadn't even been on a date yet."

"I didn't want to actually do that." Dan lifted my hand and gently kissed my knuckles. A flutter filled my belly. "I don't want to rush you. I want to take you on as many dates as you want and need. But I did want you to know where I'm headed and to make sure that's where you want to head too. We can take it as slowly as you need."

That's where I wanted to go too. All I could think when I looked at Dan—the man who loved me enough to go at the pace I needed to feel safe and who accepted me with all my baggage—

was how much I loved him in return and wanted to raise Janie together and grow old together. I never thought I'd find that.

And maybe I hadn't found it. Maybe it was a gift from God made all the more precious because I hadn't thought it possible.

Dan frowned slightly. "One thing."

The warmth I'd been feeling cooled slightly. "What?"

"Do you want me to call you Amy now? I'll do it if you want, but it'll be a challenge. When I think about you, it's always as Isabel."

I wasn't Amy anymore. I hadn't been Amy for a long time.

Amy was a woman without friends. Amy was a woman who let a man convince her she was worthless. Amy was scared.

Isabel wasn't any of those things. Isabel had a successful business and people who loved her. She knew who she was—good and bad, strengths and weaknesses—and she was brave enough to keep fighting for a better life.

I didn't want to hear the name Amy on Dan's lips. I'd been Isabel from the moment we met, and I wanted to stay Isabel until the day I died.

"Isabel," I said. "I think when I change my last name, I'll legally change my first name too. Isabel Holmes has a nice ring to it, don't you think?"

I started to smile, but before I could finish, he cut me off with a kiss.

LETTER FROM THE AUTHOR

I hope you had fun reading the conclusion of Isabel's story.

The question I know I'm going to get is "Will there ever be more stories with Isabel and Dan?"

When I first planned out this series, this book was where I saw the story ending. That said, I've learned from experience to never say never. This is the end of their story for now, but if I came up with another story I absolutely have to write for them, I will.

In the meantime, I'm already hard at work on my new series, starring a veterinarian sleuth. If you love animals the way I do, then this next series is for you.

If you want to know when the first book in my new series releases, make sure to sign up for my newsletter at https://www.subscribepage.com/maplesyrupmysteries. You'll also receive a free ebook copy of *Sapped*, the Maple Syrup Mysteries prequel novella.

And if you enjoyed this book, I'd really appreciate it if you'd leave an honest review on Amazon or Goodreads. Reviews help fellow readers know if this is a book they might enjoy. Even a short sentence helps!

Love,

Emily

RECIPE: TIRAMISU CUPCAKES

Isabel's tiramisu cupcakes have been mentioned in multiple books. It's time to share the recipe for them!

INGREDIENTS:

Cake:

- 1 1/3 cups all-purpose flour
- 1 teaspoon baking powder
- 1 teaspoon instant coffee powder
- 1/4 teaspoon salt
- 1/2 cup butter, softened
- 1/2 cup granulated sugar
- 1/2 cup brown sugar
- 2 large eggs, at room temperature
- 1 teaspoon vanilla extract

1/2 cup 2% milk, at room temperature

Soaking Syrup:

1/4 cup hot water

1 1/2 teaspoons instant coffee powder

3 tablespoons granulated sugar

Icing:

3/4 cup mascarpone cheese

1/3 cup powdered sugar, sifted

1 1/2 teaspoons instant coffee powder

3/4 cup heavy cream (35%), cold

cocoa powder, for dusting

INSTRUCTIONS:

To Make the Cupcakes:

1. Preheat the oven to 350 degrees F, and line a muffin tin with cupcake liners.

2. In a medium bowl, whisk together flour, baking powder, instant coffee powder, and salt. Set aside. These are your dry ingredients.

3. In a large bowl, beat together butter, granulated sugar, and brown sugar until light in color and fluffy. This will take about 3 minutes.

4. Add eggs one at a time, and beat well after each. (You'll

know you're ready to move on when it looks smooth.)

5. Beat in vanilla extract.

6. By hand, mix in half the dry ingredients until just combined, then mix in the milk until just combined. Finish by mixing in the remaining dry ingredients. Do not overmix.

7. Fill the cupcake liners ¾ full with the batter.

8. Bake for 16-18 minutes or until a toothpick inserted into the center comes out clean.

9. Cool the cupcakes in the pan for 10 minutes, and then remove to a wire rack. You need to make the soaking syrup before they completely cool.

To Make Soaking Syrup:

10. Mix together the hot water, instant coffee powder, and sugar until the instant coffee powder and sugar dissolve.

11. Use a fork or a toothpick to make holes in the still-warm cupcakes.

12. Brush each cupcake with the coffee syrup until you've used all the syrup up.

To Make the Frosting:

13. Place a medium bowl and the whisk of your mixer into the freezer.

14. In a separate large bowl, beat together mascarpone cheese, sugar, and instant coffee powder.

15. Remove your bowl and whisk from the freezer, and whisk the heavy cream until stiff peaks form.

16. Fold the whipped cream into the mascarpone mixture.

17. Frost cupcakes immediately.

18. Store cupcakes in the refrigerator until ready to serve. Before serving, dust the tops with cocoa powder.

Makes 12 cupcakes.

MAPLE SYRUP MYSTERIES

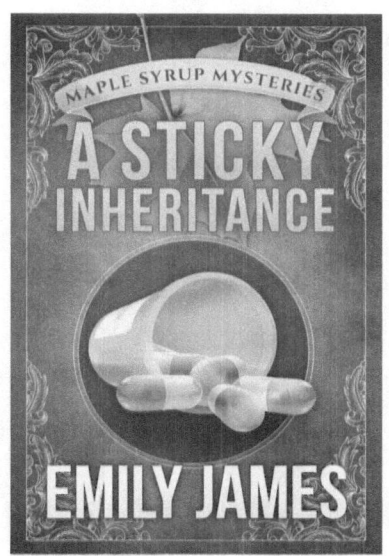

Looking for something to read next? Try Emily James' Maple Syrup Mysteries. This thirteen book series is complete and available in both print and ebook formats. The first four books are also available as audiobooks.

Criminal defense attorney Nicole Fitzhenry-Dawes thought that moving to the small Michigan tourist town of Fair Haven and taking over her uncle's maple syrup farm would keep her far away from murderers, liars, and criminals. She couldn't have been more wrong...

If you love small-town settings, quirky characters, and a dollop of romance, then you'll enjoy this amateur sleuth mystery series.

Pick up the whole series at https://smarturl.it/maplesyrupmysteries.

ABOUT THE AUTHOR

Emily James grew up watching TV shows like *Matlock, Monk,* and *Murder She Wrote.* (It's pure coincidence that they all begin with an M.) It was no surprise to anyone when she turned into a mystery writer.

Alongside being a writer, she's also a wife, an animal lover, and a new artist. She likes coffee and painting and drinking coffee while painting. She also enjoys cooking. She tries not to do that while painting because, well, you shouldn't eat paint.

Emily and her husband share their home with a blue Great Dane, a Boxer-mix, eight cats (all rescues), and a budgie (who is both the littlest and the loudest).

If you'd like to know as soon as Emily's next mystery releases, please join her newsletter list at www. subscribepage.com/cupcakes.

She loves hearing from readers.